John Cha

The Elements of Mechanical Physics

SALZWASSER
VERLAG

John Charles Buckmaster

The Elements of Mechanical Physics

1st Edition | ISBN: 978-3-75258-528-5

Place of Publication: Frankfurt am Main, Germany

Year of Publication: 2022

Salzwasser Verlag GmbH, Germany.

Reprint of the original, first published in 1864.

THE ELEMENTS

OF

MECHANICAL PHYSICS

LONDON

1864.

PREFACE.

INDUSTRY, sobriety, and quick perception, are not sufficient to make a thoughtful and intelligent workman. Without some knowledge of mathematics and mechanics he will never advance beyond the mere practical application of a few rules and principles, and he will often be driven to very circuitous methods, at a great waste of material, in arriving at results which could be obtained more easily and more readily by scientific methods. Most persons now engaged in the mechanical arts can read and write; they understand the use of tools, but they have never received that special instruction which enables a man to understand the reason of things; their muscles have been strengthened by labour, but their minds have never been disciplined by knowledge. Many mechanics possess considerable inventive talent, which frequently leads to speculations, which terminate not only in their disappointment, but in the ruin of others. If this ability (which exists to a large extent) in many of our workshops were only directed by some mathematical and mechanical knowledge, it would frequently lead to very important results. In our elementary schools we cannot expect to find much of this knowledge, and in our middle schools it is disregarded.

Within the last few years there has grown up during the winter months a very extensive system of evening classes in connexion with Mechanics' Institutions and similar bodies. Instruction in elementary science may be conveniently carried on in these classes. I have endeavoured to adapt the work for this purpose; it is popular, and at the same time demonstrative, and differs but little from other works on this subject, except in the large number of examples, most of which may be worked out by any person who understands proportion.

The principles of a science appear to me the last things understood. How many examples in arithmetic are worked before the boy can reason out the rule, and just as this power of reasoning begins to develop itself the boy leaves school, and the rule is seldom understood.

I shall be glad if teachers and others could give me any hints for the improvement of the work, or any additional examples. I must express my obligations to Mr. Aarons, of St. Mark's College, and Mr. Adkins, of Leicester, for many valuable suggestions.

St. John's Hill, Wandsworth, S.W.,
January, 1864.

THE

ELEMENTS OF MECHANICAL PHYSICS.

CHAPTER I.

THE Science of Mechanics may be conveniently studied under two divisions, *viz.*:—

STATICS, *which treats of Bodies in a State of Rest, and*

DYNAMICS, *which investigates the Laws of Bodies in Motion.*

If a person were to ask himself this question,—Why does that stone which I see on the ground remain year after year in the same position? By the consideration of this question, and others which would arise out of it, a person has commenced the study of that branch of mechanics known as Statics, or the laws which govern bodies in a state of rest.

But if that stone be thrown into the air, and the question asked why does it not continue moving for ever in a uniform straight line, or why, after a few seconds, it falls to the earth, and is again brought to a state of rest? By the consideration of these and *similar questions*, a person has commenced the study of Dynamics, or the laws which govern a body in motion.

Bodies of themselves cannot change from a state of rest to a state of motion, or from a state of motion to a state of rest.

There must be some cause to put a body at rest in motion, or to bring a body in motion to a state of rest.

FORCE.

Let us suppose a ball resting on a smooth table. If it be struck in any direction parallel to the surface of the table, it will move in the direction in which the blow was given. While in motion it may be struck again at an angle to the line in which it is moving, it will now move in a different direction.

If a blow of sufficient *magnitude* be given to the ball in a direction exactly opposite to that in which it is moving, the ball will be brought to a state of rest. In this illustration the ball was first moved from a state of rest to a state of motion; it was then struck so as to change the direction of its motion, and then brought to a state of rest. That which caused all these changes is called *force*. From this we learn that force tends to change bodies from a state of rest to a state of motion. To change the motion of bodies into different motions. To change bodies from a state of motion to a state of rest.

Definition.—Force is any cause which changes or tends to change the state of rest or motion in a body.

The direction of a force may be represented by a line, and its magnitude by a number. But when we represent magnitude by a number, we must have some *fixed* standard of the same kind as that we represent *by the number*: inches, feet, yards, &c., are the units commonly used for comparing lengths. Ounces, pounds,, tons, &c., are the units for comparing pressures or forces.

A pound pressure means that amount of force which is exerted towards the centre of the earth, by the quantity of matter called a pound.

A pound of matter is a quantity equal to 27·727 cubic inches of pure water at a temperature of 60° Fahrenheit.

A line has a great advantage over a number in representing force.

The direction of the force is shown, and the extremity or commencement of the line shows the point at which the force acts. Forces may also be represented in magnitude by lines of different lengths: a unit of length being taken to represent a unit of force. The point at which the force acts, the direction of the force, and its magnitude, may all be defined by a line, while a number can only represent its magnitude.

GRAVITATION AND WEIGHT.

If we take a stone and hold it on the hand, we feel a downward pressure which is called *weight.* The stone seems drawn towards the earth, and upon turning the hand over the stone falls to the ground. There must be some unseen force which causes the stone first to press the hand, and then to fall to the ground when the hand is withdrawn.

If a stone be thrown upwards it will rise only for a few seconds; it will then fall faster and faster until it is stopped and brought to a state of rest by the surface of the earth.

This unseen force not only caused the stone to fall *when the support of the hand was withdrawn,* but it has neutralised and overcome the upward force which was given to the stone when it was thrown into the air. That such a force exists is proved by experiment, and it is also proved that it consists of a force in the centre of the earth, which is called attraction, and all bodies are attracted or drawn in straight lines towards the earth's centre. The resistance of the ground prevents bodies moving below the surface of the earth.

This property of bodies, falling towards the earth's centre, is called *gravity*, and the effect it produces on a body, the *gravitation* of that body.

The attraction of gravitation is always operating, and will operate through all time, although its effects are not always visible; for the attraction may be neutralised by some other force. If a globe be suspended from the ceiling by a string, it does not move towards the centre of the earth, but it is, nevertheless, attracted towards it. The string is stretched; this stretching of the string is called its tension; and if the string were cut the globe would fall, because the counteracting force would no longer operate.

Every body is continually attracted towards the centre of the earth, even though it may be prevented by some obstacle from actually moving in that direction.

From this it will be understood what is meant by the term—weight.

Weight, then, is the force with which a body presses downwards towards the centre of the earth; it is, in fact, the measure of the earth's attraction.

When we say a body weighs five pounds, we mean that its pressure towards the centre of the earth is the *same* as that of five other bodies, each of whose pressures had been called by common consent a pound.

The five bodies, weighing a pound each, would bend a spring to the same extent as the one body weighing five pounds.

Force may act in any direction, but *weight* can only act vertically downwards towards the earth's centre.

ON MATTER—ITS MASS, DENSITY, AND VOLUME.

Matter is the general name of everything which occupies space.

Two bodies may be of the same size, but not of the same weight. A cubic inch of cork weighs much less than a cubic inch of lead. These two bodies contain different quantities of matter. The cork is very porous, and the particles of which it is composed are further apart, and therefore fewer of them in a given space; while in the lead the particles are crowded into a much smaller bulk, and therefore contain a greater quantity of matter.

Mass.

The whole quantity of matter contained in a body is called the *mass* of the body.

Now the *weight* of a body evidently depends upon the quantity of matter, that is, upon the *mass* of the body; and hence the *weight* of a body is said to be the measure of its *mass*. Thus, for example, the *mass* of a body weighing two pounds is *twice* the *mass* of a body weighing one pound.

The term *mass* must not be confused with *weight*, but at the same time in *comparing* the *masses* of two bodies, it will be sufficient to compare their weights:—

Thus, the masses of two bodies weighing respectively 5 lbs. and 7 lbs. will be 5 times and 7 times respectively the mass of a body weighing 1 lb., and ∴ are as 5 is to 7.

Again, if we say that the *mass* of a body is 10, we mean that it is 10 times the mass of some other body, which we have chosen as our standard; as for instance,

Suppose we agree to take the mass of a body whose weight is 12 lbs. as our unit of mass, then the mass of a body whose weight is 36 (or 3 times 12) lbs. would be 3.

Density.

By the *density* of a body is understood the closeness of the particles of which the body is composed.

In the illustration above given of a cubic inch of lead weighing more than a cubic inch of cork, it is evident that there must be more matter in the lead than the cork. The particles of matter must therefore lie closer together in the lead than in the cork, and this difference is expressed by saying the density of lead is greater than the density of cork.

The quantity of matter in a given volume of a body determines its density, and is measured by the quantity of matter contained in some unit adopted as the standard of measurement. This unit is generally a cubic inch of distilled water at a temperature of 60°.

By *mass* we understand the whole quantity of matter in a body. By *density* we mean the closeness of the particles of which that body is composed.

Volume.

The magnitude or size of a body is called its *volume, and is measured* by the number of cubic inches it contains.

CHAPTER II.

CENTRE OF GRAVITY.

EVERY solid body may be regarded as made up of particles held together by the force of cohesion.

The force of these particles may be regarded as parallel to one another, since they converge towards the earth's centre, the distance of which is very great compared with the body. Now, all these equal and parallel forces, infinite in number, may be replaced by a single force applied at a certain point, and *this point of application is called the centre of gravity of a body, or it may be regarded as the centre of parallel and equal forces.*

All bodies of uniform density and of regular geometrical form may have their centre of gravity found geometrically, but it often happens that actual experiment is necessary to find the centre of gravity of plane irregular bodies. The centre of gravity of a cone or pyramid of uniform density is $\frac{1}{4}$ of its height from the base, and every paraboloid $\frac{1}{3}$ of its height.

A boy who endeavours to balance a stick by laying it across his finger, is endeavouring to determine experimentally the centre of gravity of the stick, and when the finger is directly under the centre of gravity, or the centre of parallel and equal forces, the stick will balance, or be in equilibrium. There is only one *condition necessary*, and that is, that its centre of gravity be supported; no matter by what means this is effected, it will only be at rest when this condition is fulfilled. But if, on the contrary, it be not fulfilled, the body will incline to that direction in which its centre of gravity lies. If a body be suspended by a string it will only rest when the centre of gravity is in a vertical line with the point of suspension. This principle may sometimes be used to find the centre of gravity of an irregular body; for if strings be attached to two different points of a body, and the body be suspended by each in succession, then the vertical lines drawn through these points will intersect each other in the centre of gravity.

Stable and Unstable Equilibrium.

The stable and unstable condition of bodies which occur in every-day life, often independently of our own arrangements or contrivance, depend on the position of their centre of gravity. A waggon loaded with hay is more easily overturned than one loaded with stones, because in the one case the centre of gravity is raised considerably above the base, in the other case the centre of gravity is much lower. A tall thin man for the same reason is more easily knocked down than a short fat man. Every body stands more securely the nearer its centre of gravity is to the earth, the wider its base, and the greater its weight. Every boy knows he can stand more firmly on both legs than on one; in the former case the vertical line of direction from the centre of gravity falls between two feet, in the other it has to be brought within the base occupied by the sole of one foot. If we wish to stand very firmly, as boys do when they *fight or wrestle,* the base is enlarged by placing the feet wide apart. If a man carries a load on his back his centre of gravity is altered, and he inclines forward to bring the line of direction within the base of his feet. If a woman carries a child in one arm she leans to the opposite side, if a man carries a basket in front of him he leans backward.

When the centre of gravity is considerably elevated above the base, or where the base is very narrow, so that the vertical line from the centre of gravity falls without the base, then the body turns over, the conditions of equilibrium being no longer fulfilled. Hollow bodies, such as boxes and rings, have a centre of gravity, not within the volume of the body, but in an adjoining space. These may be supported, if any solid body be connected with them, so as to pass through their centre of gravity, and the support applied at that point the bodies will be supported. Spherical bodies of uniform density have their centre of gravity in the centre of the body. The centre of gravity of the earth is at its centre. Spherical bodies move easily on a plane surface, and their centres of gravity are in such a case always the same distance from the plane. It can, therefore, only remain at rest upon a perfectly horizontal plane; if the inclination be ever so small, the body will roll to the lowest part of the plane.

In balancing a body the centre of gravity must be supported. When a boy balances a pole on the end of his finger, he has constantly to keep moving either forwards, backwards, or sideways, to keep his fingers under the centre of gravity of the pole; and the longer the pole the more difficult the experiment. In spinning a top, a rapid rotatory motion is given by the string, and its centre of gravity is in a line with the peg, or *point upon which* it turns. When it falls, the centre of gravity tends to the lowest point, and the top falls upon its side to a state of rest.

An egg laid upon the table in the direction of its longer axis is in stable equilibrium; but if placed on its end it is in a condition of unstable equilibrium, and it is no easy task to make it stand. Sometimes the egg is shaken so as to break the membrane enclosing the yolk, which now falls lower down, and this lowers considerably the centre of gravity; if a little of the shell be now scraped off, so as to flatten the base, an egg may be made to balance on one of its ends. The heavy hands of a church-clock afford a good illustration of stable and unstable equilibrium. When the hand is at six it is in a condition of stable equilibrium, its centre of gravity is in a vertical line with the axis on which it turns, or point of suspension, and if it be removed either to the right or left it tends to fall. At twelve o'clock it is in a state of unstable equilibrium, and if it were removed either to the right or left it would not return to its previous position. From this it will be seen, that in heavy clock-hands where the centre of gravity is some distance from the axis, the clock would tend to gain from twelve to six and lose from six to twelve. There is, however, a counterweight usually attached, by making a heavy ball on the hand in an opposite direction to the pointer.

To find the centre of gravity of a material straight line of uniform density:

Let A B be the straight line, bisect it in C, C will

be the centre of gravity. From the point C, take two points equidistant from C, as D and E. The line may be considered as made up of pairs of particles placed at points D and E. But the two particles D and E balance each other on the point C, and all other pairs of particles will balance for the like reason. Therefore the point C is the centre of gravity of the whole line.

To find the centre of gravity of two heavy points joined by a rigid bar without weight:

Let A B be the two heavy points. Let W and R represent their weights. Take in A B a point such that

$$W+R : R = A\,B : A\,C$$

C will be the centre of gravity of A B

By division W : R = B C : A C. A and B will balance each other, and the pressure on C is W + R

To find the centre of gravity of a number of heavy points:

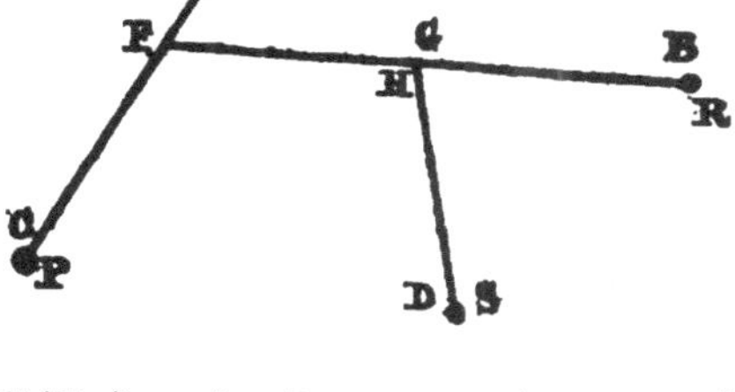

Let A B C D be the heavy points, and their weights *P Q R S*. Join C A and take a point F in C A, such

that P+R : R :: C A : A F. Join F B and take a point H in F B, such that P+Q+R : Q :: F B : F H. Join H D and take a point in H D, such that P+Q+R+S : S :: H D : H G. G will be the centre of gravity of P Q R S.

Every system of heavy points has a centre of gravity, which may always be found by the above construction.

To find the centre of gravity of a material plane triangle :

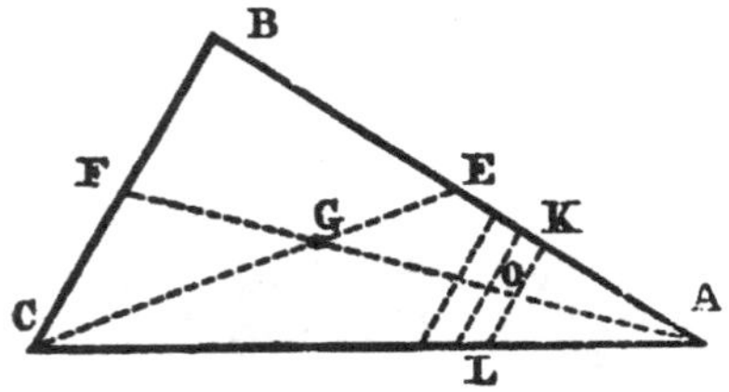

Let A B C be the triangle ; bisect A B in E and join E C, and bisect B C in F and join F A ; let G be the point of intersection of E G and F A. G is the centre of gravity of the triangle.

The triangle may be considered as made up of straight lines, K L parallel to B C ; and the centre of gravity of any one of those lines, as K L is at O in the line A F, therefore each of these lines will balance on A F ; therefore the whole triangle which is made up of these lines will balance on A F in any position, and therefore the centre of gravity of the triangle is in the line A F. In like manner the triangle may be considered as made up of straight lines, parallel to A B, and by similar reasoning the centre of gravity is in the line C E.

Therefore the centre of gravity of the triangle is *at G, the intersection* of A F and C E.

CHAPTER III.

LEVERS.

A LEVER is a rigid bar, generally of wood or iron, moveable only in one plane, about a point, which is called the fulcrum. The portions of the lever, between the fulcrum and the points where the weight and power act, are called the arms of the lever; and the lever is supposed to be without weight.

Levers are of three kinds.

In a lever of the first kind, the fulcrum, or point upon which the lever turns, is situated between the *weight*, or *resistance*, and the *power*.

In a lever of the second kind, the weight is between the fulcrum and the power.

In a lever of the third kind, the power is applied between the fulcrum and the weight.

In levers of the second and third kind, the fulcrum is generally at the end of the lever.

In every mechanical power which depends on the principle of the lever, the

Rule is—*That the moments tending to turn the lever in one direction must (to balance or be in equilibrium) be equal to the moments tending to turn it in an opposite direction.*

The moments are obtained by multiplying the weight or resistance into its distance from the fulcrum, and the power into its distance from the fulcrum. If these products are equal, the lever will balance, or be in equilibrium. The distances must be in the same denomination: inches, feet, or whatever unit is adopted; and the same with the power and the weight: ounces, pounds, or hundred-weights.

In calculating the power of the lever, if any three terms be given, the fourth can be found by proportion.

When several weights act on one side of the fulcrum, the sum of these moments is obtained by multiplying each weight into its distance from the fulcrum, then adding the products together, which will give the sum of the moments acting on one side of the fulcrum, and similarly the moments on the other side may be obtained; and if these moments are equal, the lever will be in equilibrium. When a lever is bent or curved, perpendiculars must be let fall from

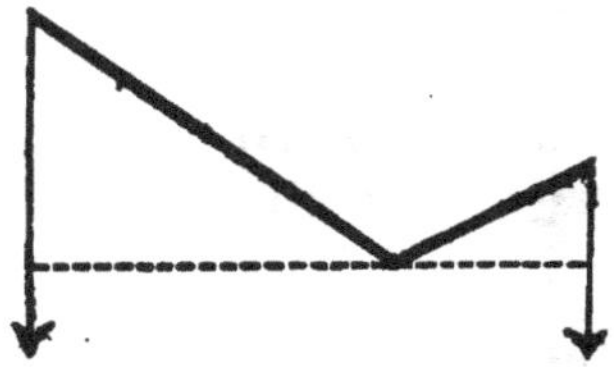

the fulcrum on lines drawn to represent the directions of the forces, as in the accompanying figure. This will bring the lever into the conditions of one with straight arms, and it may be calculated according to the rule already given.

Virtual Velocity.

In a lever with equal arms, each arm passes through the same space in the same time; it is, in fact, a balance, and has no mechanical advantage. But in levers whose arms are of different lengths, the long arm passes through a greater space than the short arm, in proportion as the weight to be overcome is greater than the power.

A small weight descending a long distance in a given time, is equal in effect to a great weight descending through a proportionally shorter space in the same time.

What is gained by raising a large weight through a small space, is lost by the power having to descend through a proportionally greater space. We may express this reasoning in another way. If the two arms of a lever be in equilibrium by having a weight of 9 lbs. at one end, three inches from the fulcrum, and a weight of 3 lbs. at the other end, and nine inches from the fulcrum, the lever will be in equilibrium, because the moments tending to turn it in one direction, $9 \times 3 = 27$, are equal to the moments tending to turn it in the opposite direction, $3 \times 9 = 27$.

If motion be given to the lever, then *the power multiplied by the vertical space through which it moves will be equal to the weight multiplied by the vertical space through which it moves*; and this principle applies not only to the lever, but to the wheel and axle, the inclined plane, the pulley, and every mechanical contrivance and arrangement. It is important that these illustrations should never be forgotten; it will often help to simplify calculations.

Balances.

Commercial balances are not unfrequently badly constructed, making one arm longer or heavier than the other. In this case the purchaser is frequently defrauded of his just weight. The fraud may, however, be easily detected.

When the substance to be weighed is in equilibrium with the weights in the other scale-pan, the substance and weights should be transposed, and if equilibrium is still obtained, the balance is true.

The shorter arm of a balance may be so heavy that there is equilibrium when the scales are empty; still the balance is false, for a weight suspended from the short arm will be in equilibrium with a less weight from the long arm.

Correct weight may be obtained by a false balance in the following manner: Determine the weight of the body alternately in each scale-pan; a mean proportional between the weights thus found will be the true weight of the body.

For example, if a body weigh 9 oz. in one scale-pan and 4 oz. in the other, 6 oz. is the true weight, for 6 is a mean proportional between 4 and 9.

$9 \times 4 = 36$. The root of which is 6.

Again, if a body weigh 7lbs. in one scale-pan and $9\frac{1}{7}$ in the other, the product of $7 \times 9\frac{1}{7} = 64$. The root of which is 8, the true weight of the body.

The Safety-Valve.

The safety-valve of a steam-engine is a lever of the third kind, and was invented by Papin. The valve consists of a metal plug, slightly conical, and fitting accurately into a hole on the top of the boiler. From the lower end of the plug a metal rod passes through a hole; the object of this is to keep the valve in a vertical position. If the arm of the valve be not loaded, the plug will remain in its seat, until the upward pressure of the steam in the boiler on the valve exceeds the pressure of the atmosphere, plus the weight of the valve; it is then lifted out of its socket, and a portion of the steam escapes, which lessens its elastic force and density in the boiler. When a greater pressure than this is required, the arm of the lever is loaded with a weight, and its distance from the fulcrum will determine for a given valve the pressure, beyond which the elastic force of the steam in the boiler cannot proceed.

Mechanical Combinations and their Advantages.

It is sometimes thought that, by levers and other mechanical contrivances, we can increase power. This is a mistake, a machine can only give out the power which is applied to it; but we may, by mechanical contrivances, manage to apply this power more advantageously. If a man has to raise a block of stone weighing 5 cwts. through a space of two feet, he would be unable to accomplish his object without some mechanical appliance; his strength would not be sufficient to lift it from the ground the same as he could lift a *brick*. But with a lever he would raise the weight through small spaces by a number of successive efforts. Suppose the stone to be raised each time one inch, bringing the cwts. to pounds, we have 560 lbs. Now this 560 lbs. raised through one inch, is equal to one pound raised through a space of 560 inches. If by a lever, or any mechanical appliance, a man raises a greater weight, he only raises it through a proportionally shorter distance.

Examples of the application of the lever are numerous.

Of the first kind, we have the thumb-latch of the door; a bar used to raise a heavy stone, by pressing down one end with the hand so as to raise the weight with the other end of the lever. The stone is the weight; the fulcrum is the brick on which the lever turns; and the power is the force of the hand. Stirring the fire when the poker rests on the bar of the grate, the see-saw of children, scissors, pincers, curling-tongs, are double levers of this kind. The pivot is the fulcrum.

Levers of the second kind: a bar used to raise a weight, by resting one end on the ground and raising the other end with the hand. The weight is between the hand and the other end of the lever; the fulcrum in this case is the ground; the power is the lifting force exerted by the hand; and the resistance by the weight. Double levers of this kind: nutcrackers, lemon-squeezers.

In levers of the third kind, the power and weight are on the same side of the fulcrum. The raising of a ladder by placing one end against a wall, or some obstacle to keep it firm; the treddle of a turning-lathe; the arm of a man. Double levers of this kind: a pair of tongs, used to hold a coal, and some kinds of shears.

If two weights, P *and* W, *acting perpendicularly on a straight lever on opposite sides of the fulcrum balance each other, then* P : W *inversely as their distances from the fulcrum, and the pressure on the fulcrum is equal to their sum.*

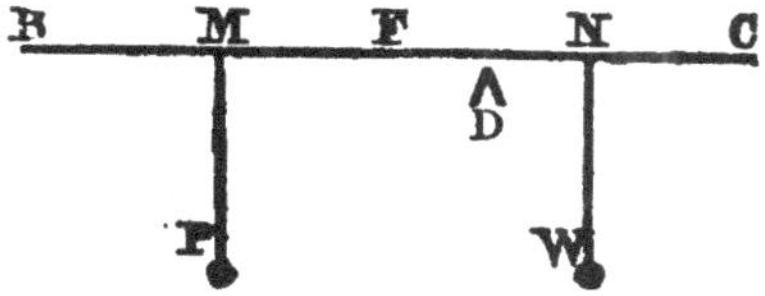

Let there be an iron rod of uniform density, whose weight may be represented as P+W. If it be placed horizontally, it will balance on a fulcrum placed at its middle point, and the pressure on this fulcrum will be P+W.

Let B C be divided in F so that

$$BF : BC :: P : P+W$$

Then since the rod B C is supposed to be of uniform density, the

Weight B F of the rod : to weight of the whole :: B F : B C :: P : P+W, by construction,

but the weight of the whole = P+W

∴ weight of the part B F = P, and

∴ weight of F C = W

But if the parts B F and F C be collected at their middle points, M and N, and act perpendicularly on the lever B C, they will produce the same effect by their weights as before. Therefore the weights P and W, acting perpendicularly at M and N, will balance about

D, the middle point of B C, and the pressure on D will be P+W.

$$\frac{P}{W}=\frac{BF}{FC}=\frac{BC-CF}{BC-BF}=\frac{2\,CD-2\,CN}{2\,BD-2\,BM}=\frac{CD-CN}{BD-BM}$$

$$=\frac{DN}{DM}$$

$$P:W=DN:DM$$

$$P\times DM=W\times DN$$

If two forces acting perpendicularly on a straight lever in opposite directions on the same side of the fulcrum balance each other, they are (1) *inversely as their distances from the fulcrum,* (2) *and the pressure on the fulcrum is equal to their difference.*

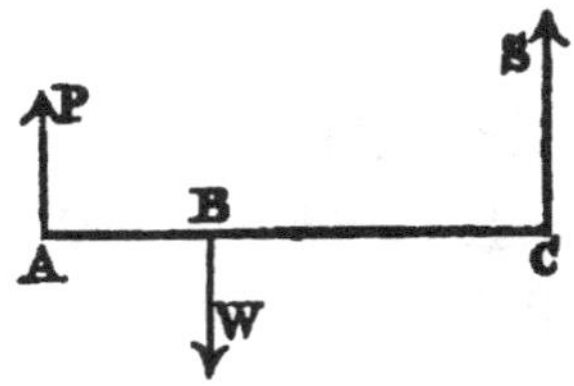

Let P and W, forces acting perpendicularly at A and B on the lever A C in opposite directions, and on the same side of the fulcrum at C, balance each other, then

$$P:W=CB:CA$$

and W being the force nearer to the fulcrum, the pressure on the fulcrum at C is W−P. Let the fulcrum at C be removed, and let its pressure S be supplied by a force equal to S, and acting perpendicularly to the lever in the direction of the force P. Since P and S are kept in equilibrium by W, they must produce a pressure at B equal and opposite to W. Let W be *removed,* and its place supplied by a fulcrum on the opposite side to that on which W acted, it will sustain the pressure W produced by P and S.

The case is now that of two forces acting perpendicularly on opposite sides of the fulcrum and balancing each other.

$$\therefore P : S = CB : BA$$

$$\therefore P : P+S = CB : CB+BA = CB : CA$$

But W, the pressure on the fulcrum, which is supposed to be placed at B, is $= P+S$.

$$\therefore P : W = CB : CA$$

$$\text{Since } W = P+S \quad \therefore S = W - P$$

If two forces acting at any angles on the arms of any lever balance each other, they are inversely as the perpendiculars drawn from the fulcrum to the directions in which the forces act.

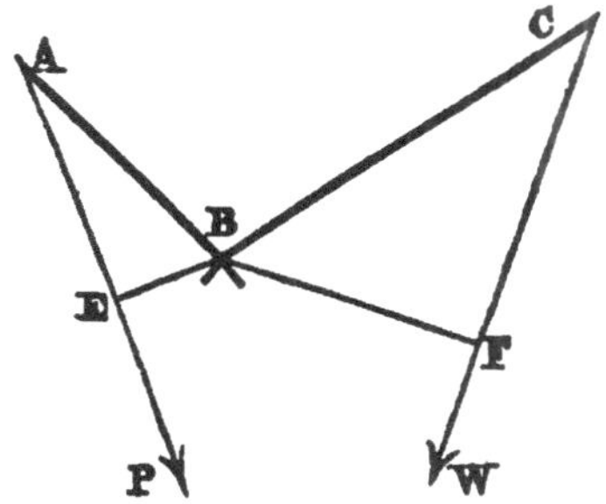

Let two forces, P and W, acting at any angles on the arms of the lever whose fulcrum is at B, balance each other, and from B draw B E, B F perpendicular to A P and C W, then shall

$$P : W = BF : BE$$

Suppose E B F to be a rigid lever without weight, the *equilibrium* is not affected. Now P may be considered to act at any point in its line of action E P. Let us suppose it acting at E, and similarly suppose W acting at F, we find the forces the same as if acting perpendicularly at E and F.

But in that case $P : W = BF : BE$

And also in the supposed case $P : W = BF : BE$

$$P \times BE = W \times FB$$

Examples.

1. The arms of a straight horizontal lever are 8 and 12; a weight of 9 lbs. is suspended at the shorter arm; what weight must be suspended at the other end to produce equilibrium? and what is the pressure on the fulcrum?

$$P \times \overset{\text{Long arm.}}{DM} = W \times \overset{\text{Short arm,}}{DN}$$

$$P \times 12 = 9 \text{ lbs.} \times 8 = 72 \text{ lbs.}$$
$$\therefore P = 72 \div 12 \text{ or } 6 \text{ lbs.}$$

2. If 69 ozs. be placed 4 inches from the fulcrum; at what distance must I place 1 lb. 14 ozs. on the other arm to produce equilibrium?

3. If 1 cwt. 3 qrs. 9 lbs. be placed at a distance of 3 inches from the fulcrum; what weight must be placed on the side at a distance of 17 inches to produce equilibrium?

4. If 6 lbs. be placed on one arm of a lever at a distance of 5 feet 9 inches; what must be the length of the other arm so that 1 cwt. may be balanced?

5. If 5505 lbs. be placed on a lever of the second kind at a distance of 6 inches from the fulcrum; at what distance from the weight must I apply 1 cwt. to produce equilibrium?

6. The length of the long arm of a lever is 69 inches, a force of 6 lbs. is applied at the extremity; what must be the length of the other arm so that 112 lbs. may be kept in equilibrium?

7. A lever of the third kind is 3 feet 6 inches long, a force of 108 lbs. is applied at a distance of 6 inches from the fulcrum; what resistance will be necessary at the other end so as to produce equilibrium?

8. If 500 ozs. be placed at a distance of 6 inches from the fulcrum; what weight must I apply at a distance of 18 inches to keep the lever in equilibrium?

9. A piece of timber projects 4 feet from the wall, at the extremity a weight of 3 cwts. is applied, the timber enters the wall 6 inches; what is the force tending to overturn the wall?

10. A scaffold-board is 12 feet long, it projects over the pudlock 3 feet; supposing a man weighing 13 stone walked to the shorter end, would the scaffold-board throw him off?

11. A man has a clawed hammer, the handle is 1 foot 3 inches long; he applies a pressure of 96 lbs.; the head of the hammer acts as a fulcrum; the nail is acted upon 2 inches from the fulcrum; what force will be applied in drawing the nail?

12. In a system of compound levers, the long arms are 4, 6, and 8 inches respectively, and the short arm 1, 2, and 3 inches; a weight of 2 ozs. is applied at the extremity of the long arm of the system; what weight must be placed at the other extremity to produce equilibrium?

13. The arms of a straight horizontal lever are 4 and 6 inches, a weight of 4 lbs. is hung at the end of the shorter arm; what weight hung at the other end will balance it?

14. The arms of a straight horizontal lever are 1

foot and 3 feet, 12 lbs. hangs at the extremity of the longer arm; what weight hung at the other end will balance it?

15. On a lever of the second kind the whole length is 2 feet 1 inch, a weight of 10 lbs. is supported, 10 inches from the fulcrum, by a force of 5 lbs. acting upwards; find the distance between the weight and the point at which the force is applied.

16. A force of 5 lbs. acts upwards on a lever of the third kind, which is 25 inches long, at a distance of 15 inches from the fulcrum; what weight must be hung at the other part to produce equilibrium?

17. Two weights, 3 lbs. and 4 lbs., balance on a lever 32 inches long; find the position of the fulcrum.

18. Two weights, 5 lbs. and 7 lbs., balance on a straight lever 32 inches long; find the position of the fulcrum.

19. The arms of a lever are 14 and 22 inches, and the pressure on the fulcrum is 36 lbs.; find the weights which balance each other at the extremities of the lever.

20. In a lever of the first kind, weights of 4 lbs., 6 lbs., 9 lbs., 12½ lbs. are placed at the following distances from the fulcrum: 3 inches, 5 inches, 7 inches, and 2 feet. What must be the length of the long arm of the lever so that a pressure of 5 lbs. shall produce equilibrium?

21. Six weights, of 9, 6, 7, 5, 12, and 8 lbs., are suspended on the long arm of a lever, which is 3 feet 6 inches long, and three weights of 96, 24, 16 lbs. on the other arm, which is 2 feet 6 inches long. The first six weights are arranged at the following distances from the fulcrum: 3 feet, 4 feet 6½ inches, 9 feet, 13 feet, 2 feet 6 inches. The other weights at 6 feet, 9 feet, 2 feet 6 inches from the fulcrum. Will the lever be in equilibrium?

22. A lever of the first kind is acted on by five forces, three forces of 50, 28, and 40 act on one side of the fulcrum at the following distances: 2, 3, and 5. The other two forces are 84 and 100, placed at the following distances: 1 and 3. Will the lever be in equilibrium?

23. The short arm of a lever is 5 inches, and the long arm 60 inches. What weight on the long arm will balance 1 cwt. on the short arm?

24. Two walls 9 feet apart support a beam; a pig weighing 27 stone is hung 4 feet from one wall. What is the pressure on each wall?

25. Two men carry a weight of 6 stone by means of a pole 7 feet long resting on their shoulders; one man supports a weight of 24 lbs. Find the position of the weight.

26. A weight of 17 lbs. balances a weight of 79 lbs. on the short arm of the lever, which is 17 inches. What is the length of the other arm?

27. Forces of 4 lbs. and 14 ozs. balance at the opposite arms of a lever 36 inches long. How far from the fulcrum does the greater force act?

28. Two weights 6 lbs. and 6 ozs. balance on a lever whose longer arm is four feet. What is the length of the shorter arm?

29. A weight of 20 lbs. is hung on a lever 30 inches from the end at which the fulcrum is placed. How far from the weight must a force of 12 lbs. be applied to support it?

30. A man has to raise a piece of timber with a crowbar 5 feet long; at a distance of 3 inches from one end he places a brick to act as a fulcrum, he then applies a pressure at the other end of 2½ cwts., which just raises the timber. What is its weight?

31. Two men carry a ladder; two pails, one of cement and the other of lime, are hung so as to divide

the ladder into three equal parts; the cement is twice as heavy as the lime. Compare the pressures felt by each man.

31 (*a*). Two men carry a ladder; two pails, one of cement and the other of lime, are hung so as to divide the ladder into three equal parts; the cement is three times as heavy as the lime. Compare the pressures felt by each man.

32. If 3 qrs. 18 lbs. be suspended on a lever 7 feet from the fulcrum; what weight suspended 8½ feet on the other side of the fulcrum will balance it?

33. The great beam of a steam-engine is 16 feet long, the piston acts on one end with a pressure of 2 tons at a distance of 7 feet from the fulcrum. What force will be applied to the crank turning the fly-wheel at the other end of the beam?

34. Two men work at a double-acting force-pump; the length of each lever is 36 inches; at a distance of 3 inches from the fulcrum the pistons of the pump are attached. The men exert a united force of 3 cwts. What is the force with which each piston descends?

35. At what distance from the fulcrum must 3½ lbs. be placed so as to produce equilibrium with a weight of 126 lbs. at a distance of 2½ inches from the fulcrum?

36. Weights of ½ lb. and 6 ozs. balance on a straight lever of which the longer arm is 1 foot. What is the length of the lever?

36 (*a*). Weights of 2½ lbs. and 2¼ lbs. balance on a straight lever of which the longer arm is 1 yard. What is the length of the lever?

37. On a straight lever of the second kind a force of 3 lbs. acts perpendicularly to it, and supports a *weight of 4 lbs.*, which is hung 1 foot from the ful-

crum. Find the distance from the fulcrum at which the force acts.

38. The arms of a straight lever are 14 inches and 20 inches; a weight of 3 lbs. is suspended at the longer arm. What weight must be attached to the shorter arm to produce equilibrium?

39. The arms of a lever of the second kind are 12 and 18 inches; a weight of 4 lbs. is placed at the extremity of the longer arm. What pressure must be applied at the extremity of the other arm to produce equilibrium?

40. Two men carry a barrel of beer on a pole; the barrel is 3 feet from one man and 4 feet from the other; the barrel weighs 1 cwt. What pressure does each man sustain?

40 (*a*). Two men carry a barrel of beer on a pole; the barrel is 5 feet from one man and 3¼ feet from the other, and weighs ½ cwt. What pressure does each man sustain?

41. On a horizontal beam 12 feet long with both ends supported, where must a weight be placed so that the pressure on the supports will be as 5 to 3?

41 (*a*). On a horizontal beam 1 yard long, with both ends supported, where must a weight be placed so that the pressure on the supports will be as 4 to 1½?

42. In a lever of the first kind three weights, one of 6 lbs. 5 inches from the fulcrum, one of 4 lbs. 9 inches from the fulcrum, and one of 20 ozs. 3 feet from the fulcrum. At what distance from the fulcrum must a weight of 3 lbs. be placed to produce equilibrium?

43. A straight rod 32 inches long rests in a horizontal position between two fixed pivots placed at a distance of three inches apart; one of the pivots being at the end of the rod, a weight of 8 lbs. is suspended

at the other end. What is the pressure on each pivot?

43 (*a*). A straight rod 1 yard long rests in a horizontal position between two fixed pivots placed at a distance of 26 inches apart; one of the pivots being at the end of the rod, a weight of 1 lb. is suspended at the other end. What is the pressure on each pivot?

44. Which will cut more easily, a pair of garden shears 3 feet long with a rivet 5 inches from the point, or a pair 2 feet long with a rivet $3\frac{1}{2}$ inches from the point?

44 (*a*). Which will cut more easily, a pair of garden shears $2\frac{1}{3}$ feet long with a rivet $1\frac{1}{4}$ inches from the point, or a pair 1 yard long with a rivet of one quarter of a foot? Give the reasoning by which you arrive at the answer.

45. Two boys play at see-saw on a plank 10 feet long; one boy weighs 96 lbs. the other weighs 83 lbs. How far from each boy must the fulcrum be so that they may balance each other?

45 (*a*). Two boys play at see-saw on a plank 15 feet long; one boy weighs 1 cwt. and the other 90 lbs. How far from each boy must the fulcrum be so that they may balance each other?

46. To what kind of levers do the following belong: A man wheeling a loaded barrow, a milkman with a yoke across his shoulders and a can hanging on each side, a man riding in a gig, when his weight is before the wheel and when it is behind?

47. In a lever of the second kind the weight is 28 lbs., and suspended 6 inches from the fulcrum; what must be the length of the arm at which a power of 4 ozs. is applied to produce equilibrium?

48. In a pair of steelyards if the distance of the weight from the fulcrum be $\frac{1}{10}$ of the distance of the

power from the fulcrum; what power must be applied to raise a weight 3 tons.

49. The arms of a straight horizontal lever of the first kind are 12 inches and 18 inches respectively, and the weight on the extremity of the shorter arm is 3 lbs. Determine the pressure on the fulcrum.

50. On a lever of the first kind, what power 6 feet from the fulcrum will balance 1 cwt. $4\frac{1}{2}$ feet from it?

51. In a lever on the same side of the fulcrum two weights of 3 and 5 balance. Half the sum of their distances from the fulcrum being 8, find the lengths of the arms.

52. In a lever 45 inches long resting on each end, on what point must a weight be applied so that the pressure on each end is as 5 to 4?

53. Two porters carry a piece of stone weighing 448 lbs., by means of a pole resting on the shoulders. Both men are the same height, and the weight is placed at a distance of $\frac{2}{7}$ of the pole from one of the porters. What weight does each man sustain?

53 (*a*). Two porters carry a piece of stone weighing 3 cwts. by means of a pole resting on their shoulders. Both men are of the same height, and the weight is placed at a distance of $\frac{2}{3}$ of the pole from one of the porters. What weight does each man sustain?

54. In a straight horizontal lever a force of 3 lbs. acts vertically upwards. At what point must a weight of 12 lbs. be placed to produce equilibrium round a fulcrum at the other end?

55. A body is weighed in a false balance, and in one scale appears to be 9 ozs., in the other 12 ozs. What is its true weight?

55 (*a*). A body is weighed in a false balance, and in one scale appears to be 7 ozs., in the other $9\frac{1}{4}$ ozs. What is its true weight?

56. Two weights, 6 and 9, balance on a lever 36 inches long. What distance is the fulcrum from each of the weights?

56 (*a*). Two weights, 5 and 8, balance on a lever 1 foot long. What distance is the fulcrum from each of the weights?

57. What is the length of a lever when a weight of 8 ozs. and 1 lb. balance, the longer arm of the lever being 13 inches?

58. Two weights, 7 lbs. and 5 lbs., are suspended at the ends of a straight lever 12 inches long; a force of 6 lbs. acts vertically upwards at the middle point. Where is the position of the fulcrum?

58 (*a*). Same question, but with the force 6 lbs. acting vertically downward.

58 (*b*). Two weights, 7 lbs. and 5 lbs., are suspended at the ends of a straight lever 12 inches long and 6 lbs. in weight. Find the position of the fulcrum, taking the weight of the lever into account.

58 (*c*). Two weights, 9 lbs. and 12 lbs., are suspended at the ends of a straight lever 1 yard long and 1 lb. in weight. Find the position of the fulcrum, taking the weight of the lever into account.

59. Two forces, P and R, whose directions make equal angles with the arms of a bent lever; the lengths of the arms are 8 and 12 inches, P acting at the shorter arm. Find the relation between P and R when the lever is in equilibrium.

CHAPTER IV.

THE WHEEL AND AXLE.

We have seen that a lever acts by a series of short intermittent efforts. When the weight has been raised a certain distance it must be supported, and the lever again adjusted for another effort.

The wheel and axle is a contrivance for rendering the action of a lever continuous; it may be considered as an endless succession of levers, equal to one another, and all acted on in the same manner by the power and the resistance.

The wheel and axle may be modified in a variety of ways. It sometimes consists of spokes fastened to an axle, supported either horizontally or vertically. Sometimes there is merely an axle and a winch. This arrangement is frequently employed to raise water in country districts. The length of the windlass constitutes the radius of a wheel. The axis is sometimes vertical, as in the capstan of a ship for raising the anchor; but in the wheel used for steering the ship it is horizontal.

A small cog-wheel is sometimes fitted up on an horizontal axis; the wheel is worked with a windlass, and the cogs work into a vertical rack. Such an arrangement is called the rack and pinion, and is used on canals to raise the flood-gates.

The wheel and axle consists of two cylinders of dif-

ferent diameters joined together, and having a common axis upon which it turns.

The larger cylinder is called the wheel, and the smaller the axle.

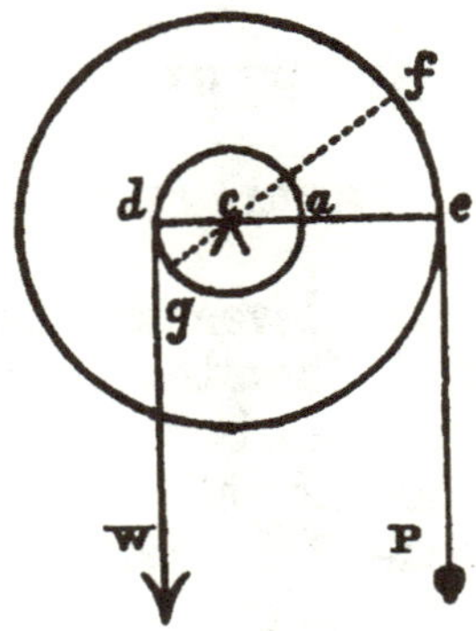

The figure represents a section of the wheel and axle, having a common centre *c*; *c e* is the radius of the wheel; *c d* is the radius of the axle; P and W are the power and resistance, acting perpendicularly downwards. Now it is evident from this that we have a lever of the first kind; the centre is the fulcrum, the radius of the axle *c d* the short arm, and the radius of the wheel *c e* the long arm, and P and W the power and resistance.

There is equilibrium in the wheel and axle when the power is to the weight, as the radius of the axle is to the radius of the wheel.

P : W = radius of axle : to radius of wheel; that is,

$$P : W = c\,d : c\,e$$

Suppose the cords by which the power and the weight are suspended to be in the plane of the same circle. Since the cylinders have a common axis, the circular ends of the wheel and axle have a common centre. Let *c* be the centre; join *c* with *d* and *e*, the points at which the cords leave, and therefore touch the circumferences of the two circles; *c d* and *c e* are therefore perpendicular to *e* P and *d* W, the lines in which the power and weight act.

Now P and W act perpendicularly to the lines *c e* and *c d*, and balance each other. Supposing *e c d* to be a lever kept at rest round *c* as the fulcrum:

$$P : W = c\,d : c\,e$$

When, therefore, this ratio of the power to the weight is fulfilled, there will be equilibrium in the wheel and axle:

If P and W be put in motion, P : W = W's velocity : to P's velocity

Let the wheel and axle be put in motion round the axis *c*, so that *f c g* becomes the horizontal diameter. P will now act at *f*, and W will act at *g*, and the velocities of P and W will be as *f e* to *d g*. P has descended through a space equal to the length of the cord *f e*, in the same time that W has ascended through a space equal to *g d*:

$$P \times f\,e = W \times d\,g$$

Examples.

1. The radius of the wheel is to that of the axle as 3 to 1. What weight will a power of 12 lbs. raise?

P : W = radius of axle : to radius of wheel.

2. The ratio of the power to the weight is as 2 : 7. The radius of the wheel is 21 inches. Find the radius of the axle.

3. What force must a man exert on the handle of a

windlass 2 feet 4 inches long, the radius of the axle being 4 inches, to overcome a resistance of 280 lbs.?

4. A flood-gate to which a cogged rack is attached weighs 6 cwt., and the resistance due to the water is 15 cwt. Supposing the windlass to have a radius of 1 foot 6 inches, and the pinion to have a radius of 2 inches; what force must be applied to raise the flood-gate?

5. An anchor weighs 26 cwt. 14 lbs., and is raised by means of a capstan, worked by six sailors. If the radius of the capstan be 12 inches, and the length of the levers 6 feet from the axis to the point where the pressure is applied; what force must each sailor exert?

6. If a capstan, 15 inches in diameter, were worked by levers 46 inches long, and the weight of the anchor 4096 lbs.; what would be the average force employed by six men in raising the anchor?

7. The radius of a winch is 1 foot 9 inches, and a power of 8 lbs. supports 56 lbs. What is the radius of the axle?

8. The power and weight of a wheel and axle act in opposite directions. The radius of the wheel is four times the radius of the axle. If the weight is 112 lbs., what power is necessary to produce equilibrium?

9. In a wheel and axle, in which the power and weight act in opposite directions, and produce a pressure on the axis equal to 10 lbs., the radius of the axle is 3 inches, and that of the wheel 5 inches; find the power and the weight?

10. A block of stone weighing 36 cwts. is raised by means of a lever 3 feet 6 inches in length projecting from an axle 9 inches in diameter. What power must be exerted to raise the stone; and, supposing each man's power equal to 108 lbs., how many men must be employed?

11. A boy raises a bucket of water weighing 56 lbs. from a well by means of a windlass 1 foot 9 inches long, attached to a wooden axle 6 inches in diameter. What power does the boy exert to raise the bucket, neglecting the doubling back of the cord on the axle?

12. If a weight of 96 lbs. balance on a wheel and axle with a power of 9 lbs., if the radius of the wheel be 20 inches, what is the radius of the axle?

13. A power of 12 lbs. balances a weight of 296 lbs. on a wheel and axle. What is the radius of the wheel if the radius of the axle be 3 inches?

14. A weight of 2 cwts. is supported by a power of 32 lbs. acting on the circumference of a wheel 2 feet 4 inches in diameter. What is the radius of the axle?

15. Twelve men, each exerting a force of 47 lbs., move the capstan with levers 7 feet 6 inches long, the radius of the axle is 1 foot 3 inches. What weight will the men sustain?

16. After some time the rope covers the whole length of the capstan, and it now begins to double back on itself, the diameter of the axle is thus increased by 3 inches. In what proportion will the power be diminished?

17. A flood-gate weighing 24 cwts. is raised by a rack and pinion; the winch is 1 foot 9 inches long, and the pinion $2\frac{1}{2}$ inches in diameter. What force must be exerted to raise the flood-gate?

18. If the radius of a wheel be 2 feet 6 inches, and the radius of the axle 3 inches; what force will be required to raise a weight of 300 lbs.?

19. The radius of a pinion working in a rack is $1\frac{1}{2}$ inches, the radius of the winch is 1 foot 3 inches. If a man exert a force of 56 lbs., what weight will he raise?

20. What power is required to raise a tub of coals weighing 4 cwts. by means of a wheel and axle when the diameter of the axle is 6 inches and the radius of the wheel 1 foot 10 inches?

21. If a power of 75 lbs. be exerted perpendicularly on the circumference of a wheel 2 feet 10 inches in diameter; what weight must be suspended on the circumference of an axle with a radius of 1½ inches to produce equilibrium?

22. The handle of a winch is 1 foot 9 inches, the radius of the axle 1½ inches. What force must a man exert to raise a weight of 500 lbs.

23. The anchor of a barge weighs 18 cwts., and is raised by a windlass with levers 3 feet 6 inches long, projecting from a horizontal axis 6 inches in diameter. Suppose two men to be employed in raising the anchor, what power must each man exert?

24. The diameter of the large wheel is 60 inches, the diameter of the axle 5 inches. What power must be applied at the large wheel to balance 112 lbs?

25. The radius of an axle is 1½ inches. What must be the radius of the wheel so that 24 lbs. may balance 2 cwt.?

26. If P=50 lbs. and W=500 lbs., what is the ratio between the radius of the axle and the radius of the wheel?

27. If a force of 76 lbs. be exerted at the extremities of each of the six arms of a capstan, each arm being 4 feet 6 inches long, and the radius of the axle 7½ inches, what is the greatest weight which could be raised?

28. If W=1296, and the radii of the wheel and axle be 16 inches and 3½ inches respectively, what does P equal?

29. If a force exerted at P=20 lbs. raises a weight

of 196 lbs. on a wheel and axle, the radius of the axle being $2\frac{1}{2}$ inches; what is the radius of the wheel?

THE COMPOUND WHEEL AND AXLE.

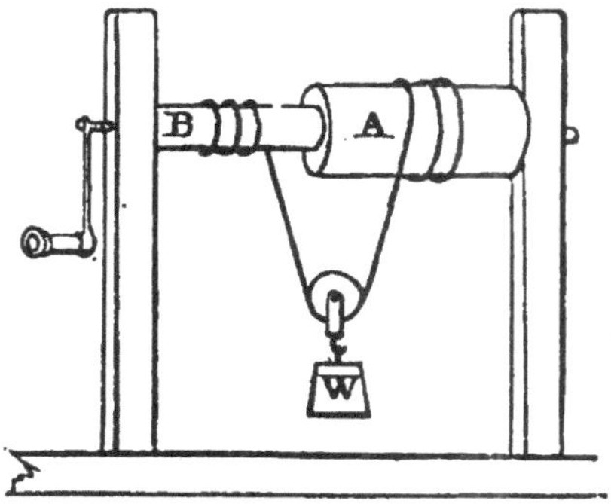

The principle of this machine is similar to the one previously described; it consists of an axle having different diameters. The two portions of the cord by which the moveable pulley and weight are supported, is wound one round the large axle and the other the opposite way round the small. When the machine is put in motion, the cord uncoils from the smaller axle B and lets down the weight which is coiled up by the larger axle A. If the two parts of the axle were of the same diameter, the length of rope coiled up would be the same as that let down, in which case the weight would neither ascend nor descend. The nearer these diameters approach each other, the less the mechanical advantage or the space through which the weight will ascend, and since the ratio of these diameters may be diminished to any extent, there is no limit to the power of this machine but the strength of the materials of which it is made.

CHAPTER V.

THE PULLEY.

The lever, the inclined plane, and the wheel and axle are constructed of rigid materials. Force is sometimes transmitted by means of a cord, and as it is often necessary to change the direction of motion, this is done by passing cords or bands over revolving wheels or pulleys.

No mechanical advantage is gained by a simple pulley. Suppose B D to be a pulley moveable about a fixed axis C. The centre of motion C is the fulcrum, the two radii of the wheel C B and C D are the equal arms of a lever, and if 4 lbs. has to be raised at W, 4 lbs. must be applied at P, and W will ascend through the same vertical space as P will descend. The cord then might have been passed through a perfectly smooth ring fixed to the ceiling with just the same advantage as passing it over a pulley.

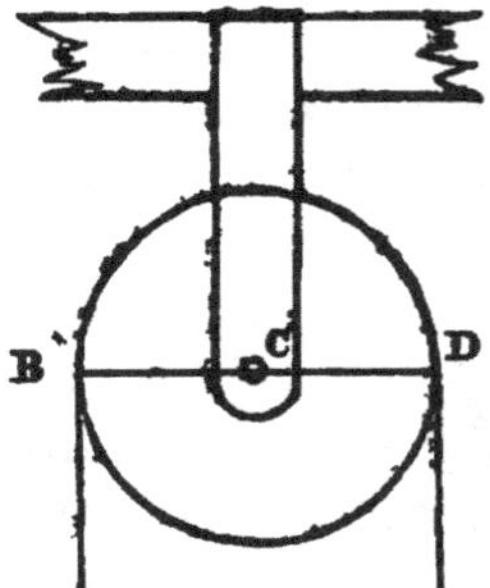

The pulley, revolving round the centre, removes in a great degree the effects of the friction on the rope, which is always considerable in the best-constructed system of pulleys. The pulley is usually made of hard wood, and sometimes of brass, and is supported in a frame called the block. Pulleys are of two kinds:

Fixed pulleys, which remain in the same position;

Moveable pulleys, which rise and fall with the weight.

The pulley, then, is a small wheel turning on its axis, usually in a framework called a block. The wheel has a grooved edge to allow the cord to pass over.

(1)

In a single fixed pulley there is equilibrium when the power and weight are equal.

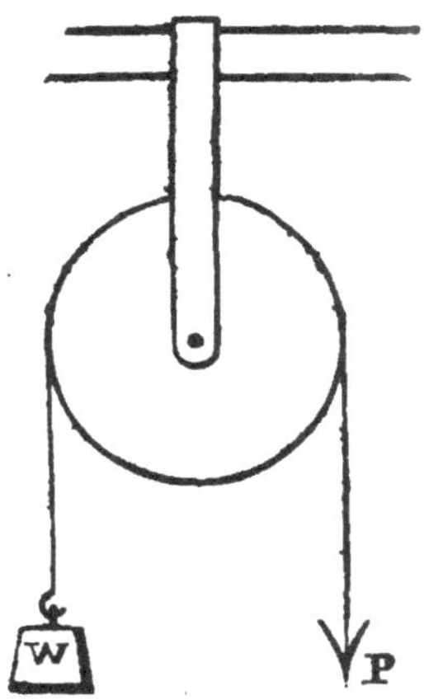

For since P and W act on the same cord, they must be equal, or motion would ensue, as the greater of the two would overcome the lesser:

$$\therefore P = W$$

(2)

In the single moveable pulley where the cords are parallel, there is equilibrium when the power is to the weight as 1 *to* 2 :

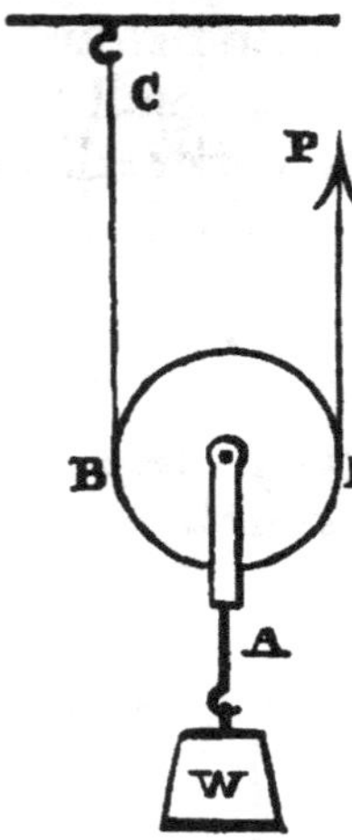

The tension of the cord P D B C, is the same throughout, and therefore equals the force applied at the extremities P.

And the tension of the cord A W = W

But the tension of A W is resisted by the tensions of D P and B C, that is tension of A W = tension D P + tension of B C

$$\text{or } W = P + P$$
$$= 2P$$
$$\therefore P : W = 1 : 2$$

If the cord P pass over a fixed pulley, still the equation remains.

(3)

In a system in which the same cord passes round any number of pulleys, and the parts of the cord between the pulleys are parallel, there is equilibrium when the power is to the weight as 1 *is to the number of strings at the lower block.*

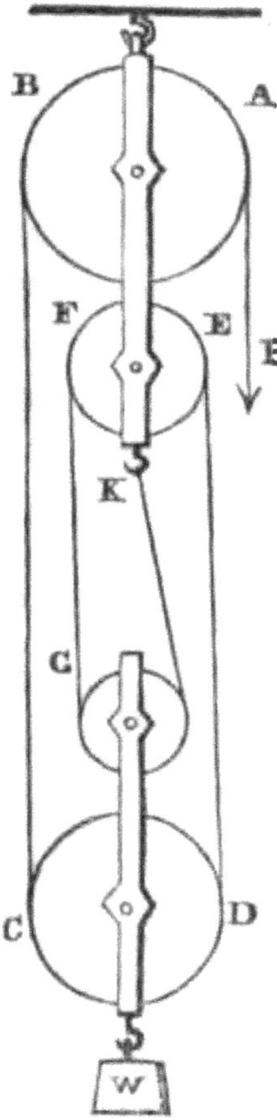

Let the figure represent a system in which the cords A B, C D, E F, G K, passes round all the pulleys and is fastened to the block K. Since there is equilibrium, the tension of the cord is the same throughout, and therefore equals the force applied at the extremity, *P*. *But W* is supported by the united tensions of the cords at the lower block, and therefore is equal to the sum of these tensions:

If there are	2	cords at the	lower block	$W = P + P =$	$2P$
,,	3	,,	,,	$W =$	$3P$
,,	4	,,	,,	$W =$	$4P$
,,	n	,,	,,	$W =$	nP

(4)

In a system in which each pulley hangs by a separate cord, and the cords are parallel, there is equilibrium when P : W : : 1 : *that power of* 2 *whose index is the number of moveable pulleys.*

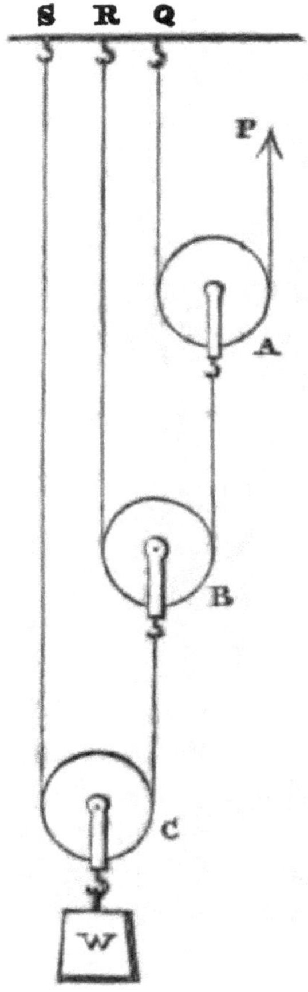

In this system the cord at which the power acts passes round a moveable pulley A, and is fixed at Q. To the block of this pulley A another cord is fixed, which passes round the pulley B and is fastened at R, and so on with any number of pulleys.

The weight is attached to the block of the lowest pulley. Since there is equilibrium the tension of the cord P A Q is the same throughout—viz. P.

And tension of cord A B = tension of A P + tension of A Q

$$= P + P$$
$$= 2 P$$

And similarly it may be shown that the tension of the cord A B R is the same throughout, and

$\therefore$ tension of B C $= 2 \times$ tension of A B $= 2 \times 2 P$
$$= 2^2 P$$
tension of C W $= 2 \times$ tension of B C $= 2 \times 2^2 P$
$$= 2^3 P$$
that is $W = 2^3 P$.

If there are 4 pulleys $W = 2^4 P$
If there are 5 pulleys $W - 2^5 P$
If there are n pulleys $W = 2^n P$

that is $P : W = 1 : 2^n$

= 1 : that power of 2 whose index is the number of moveable pulleys

Examples.

1. In system (4) there are four moveable pulleys, and a power of 6 oz. is applied; what weight is supported?

Here $P = 6$ oz. and $n = 4$
$$W = 2^n P$$
$$= 2^4 \times 6 = 16 \times 6 = 96 \text{ oz.}$$

2. In system (3) a power of 3 oz. supports a weight of 3 lbs.; what is the number of strings at the lower block?

$$\text{Here } P=3 \text{ oz. } W=48 \text{ oz. or } 3 \text{ lbs.}$$
$$\text{Now } W=n\,P$$
$$i.\,e.\ 48=n\times 3=3\,n$$
$$\therefore n=16$$

2 (*a*). A set of three moveable pulleys has a power of 6 lbs. applied. What weight will keep the system in equilibrium?

3. What power would be required to raise 332 lbs. with three moveable pulleys?

4. Six sailors with a block and tackle containing nine moveable pulleys are required to raise a sail. Suppose each man's strength represented by 2 cwts., and $\frac{2}{3}$ of the power lost by friction; what is the weight of the sail?

5. A weight of 1800 lbs. is raised by six moveable pulleys. If $\frac{2}{3}$ is lost by friction, what power will be necessary to sustain the weight?

6. In a system of pulleys (3) where the same string passes round all the wheels, and the parts of it are parallel, and supposing ten strings at the lower block; what power must be applied to sustain a weight of 1000 lbs.?

7. What weight will be raised by a power of 80 lbs. by means of two moveable pulleys, each pulley weighing 3 lbs.?

8. A power of 3 lbs. is applied to raise a weight of 36 lbs. How many pulleys must be used, neglecting the loss by friction?

9. Two pulleys are fixed—two moveable. What weight will a power of 12 lbs. sustain?

10. The power in one fixed pulley and one moveable

has descended 20 feet. What height has the weight ascended?

11. A stone weighing 3 tons is raised by means of a derrick, from which are suspended three moveable pulleys. Now suppose each man exerted a power of 2 cwt., and $\frac{2}{3}$ of the power lost by friction, how many men would it require to raise the weight? Suppose one horse equal to eight men, how many horses would it require?

12. A system of four fixed and four moveable pulleys the power descends 18 feet. What height has the weight ascended?

13. The weight in a system of three fixed and three moveable pulleys has ascended 3 feet. What space has the power descended?

14. Three fixed and three moveable pulleys raise a weight of 56 lbs. Required the power, neglecting friction.

15. In a system of three pulleys, each suspended by a separate string, a weight of x lbs. is placed at the third, and one of $3x$ lbs. at the second pulley. What is the power, neglecting friction?

16. What is the power gained by one moveable pulley?

17. A system of four moveable pulleys, and one fixed, sustains a weight of 1 ton. What is the power?

18. In a system of pulleys five are fixed and four moveable. What weight will a power of 17 lbs. support?

19. A system of five moveable pulleys is attached to a beam. Supposing a weight of $\frac{3}{4}$ of a ton to be raised; what must be the power, allowing $\frac{2}{3}$ for loss of power by friction?

20. A weight of 100 lbs. is suspended from the block of a single moveable pulley, and the end of the

string at which the power acts is fastened at the distance of 2 feet from the fulcrum of a lever of the second kind, 5 feet long. What force must be applied at the end of the lever to produce equilibrium?

21. In a system of three moveable pulleys, the weight of each pulley is 1 lb.; what power must be exerted to keep them from falling?

22. In a system in which one pulley is fixed and moveable; what power would be necessary to raise 144 lbs., and through what space would the power descend?

23. In a system in which the same string passes round four pulleys; what power would be required to raise 144 lbs.?

24. Three pulleys hang by a separate string. What power is required to raise 4 cwt.?

25. If in a system of pulleys, each hanging by a separate string, a power of 42 lbs. supports 3 cwts.; what is the number of moveable pulleys?

26. In a system of three moveable pulleys with one cord, a power of 3 lbs. is applied; what weight will be supported?

27. Suppose the power to be 8½ lbs., and the number of moveable pulleys three; what weight could be supported?

28. How many moveable pulleys would be required that a weight of 320 lbs. may be supported by a weight of 10 lbs.?

29. In a system of six moveable pulleys, if P and W be respectively 10 lbs. and 600 lbs.; will the system be the equilibrium? If not, in what direction will motion take place?

30. What power will be required to keep in equilibrium a system where there are five moveable pulleys, *and the weight is* 3360 lbs.?

31. In a system where each pulley hangs by a separate cord, and the cords are parallel, there are five pulleys; what weight will a power of 10 lbs. support?

WHEELS AND PINIONS.

The usual plan by which power is transmitted by wheel-work, is by means of cogs or teeth raised on the circumference of the wheels. The cogs on the surface of the wheels are generally called teeth, and those on the surface of the axle are called leaves; when the axle is furnished with leaves, it is called a pinion.

Wheels with teeth or cogs are of three kinds, according to the position of the teeth.

When the teeth are perpendicular to the axis they are called spur-wheels, or spur-gear.

When the teeth are parallel with the axis they are called crown-wheels.

When they are raised on a surface inclined to the axis, they are called bevelled-wheels.

The motion produced by wheels may be varied in direction by a suitable arrangement of cog-wheels. Every separate wheel on axle may be regarded as a lever, and a combination of these wheels must be regarded as a combination of levers; but as the circumference of a circle bears a constant ratio to its diameter, or radius, the circumference of any wheel may be taken as the long arm of the lever, and the circumference of the axle on which it acts as the short arm.

As the teeth must all be of equal size to work in with each other, the number of teeth in the circumference may be taken as the measure of the circumference. The number of teeth in the circumference of the large wheel may be taken as the long arm, and the number of teeth in the pinion as the short arm. Or in a train of wheels so arranged, the condition of equilibrium is the same as in a system of compound levers; that is:—*The power is to the resistance as the continued product of the radii of the pinions or the short arms of the levers is to the continued product of the radii of the wheels or the long arms of the levers.*

Examples.

1. If the radii of three pinions be expressed by the numbers 2, 3, and 4, and the radii of three wheels by the numbers 20, 25, and 30, then the power will be to the resistance as $2 \times 3 \times 4$ is to $20 \times 25 \times 30 = 15{,}000$, or a power of 24 at the first wheel will keep in equilibrium a weight of 15,000 at the last wheel.

2. A power of 5 lbs. acting at the circumference of a wheel whose radius is 5 feet, supports a weight of 200 lbs. applied at the circumference of the pinion. What is the radius of the pinion?

3. The radii of three wheels are 23, 30, and 40, and the radii of the pinions, 4, 5, and 6. What power must be applied at the circumference of the wheel to keep in equilibrium a weight of 2000 lbs.?

4. In a system of wheels and pinions driven by hands there are four wheels, the radii of which are respectively 30, 23, 53, and 58, and the four powers are 7, 12, 10, and 13. What is the ratio of the weight to the power?

5. The radius of the axle of a windlass is 3 inches, and the radius of the crank-arm 15 inches. What power must be applied to the crank-handle to support a resistance of 180 lbs. applied to the circumference of the axle?

6. In a crane the radius of the crank-arm is 25 inches, and the radius of the pinion $3\frac{1}{2}$ inches; in the second wheel the radius is $15\frac{1}{2}$ inches, and the

pinion 3 inches. If the strength of the person turning the crank-arm is equivalent to 170 lbs., what weight will he be able to raise, neglecting friction?

CRANKS AND FLY-WHEELS.

Wheels are a very important part of most machines, and are applied in a variety of ways. When they are fixed to an axle their mechanical power is always in the same proportion, that is, as the circumference of the wheel exceeds that of the axle, so much will be the increase of power. The larger the wheel and the smaller the axle, the greater will be the power; there is, of course, a limit to this, depending on the strength of the materials.

Cranks.

Cranks are frequently connected with the axle of a wheel, either to give motion or receive motion. A crank is formed by twice bending at right angles the axle. They are, in fact, a double winch.

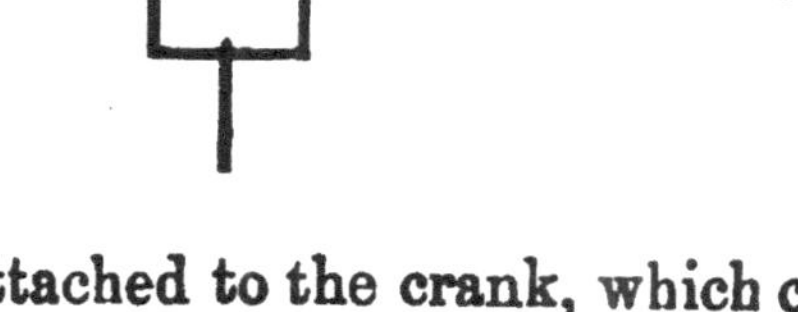

A rod is attached to the crank, which communicates with other parts of the machine. There are two positions in the revolution of a crank, in which the rod can have no effect, viz., when the rod is in the same straight line with the crank, that is, when it is at its highest and lowest points, and these are called the dead points. Were it not for the inertia of the machinery to carry the crank over these points, the machine would become stationary. Cranks are used in the foot-lathe, worked by a treddle, also in razor grinding, and are exceedingly useful in changing a rectilinear motion into a circular motion or the converse.

Fly-wheels.

Fly-wheels are generally made of metal, with a very heavy circumference. Secured by spokes to an axle, in the stationary steam-engine these wheels are sometimes of enormous size. In the locomotive engine the driving wheel answers the purpose of a fly-wheel. The motion communicated to these wheels is most frequently applied to a cranked axle, and when once set in motion they continue to revolve for some time by the inertia of the mass of metal at the circumference. They do not increase the power of the machine, but they equalise its motion, which would otherwise be a series of jerks. Fly-wheels are especially useful in connexion with cranks. The momentum which has been given to the wheel carries the axle and crank over the dead points with a velocity very little less than that which it had when the crank was in the most favourable position to be acted upon by the moving power. The principal objection to large fly-wheels is the great amount of resistance due to the friction on the axle. Thus, a fly-wheel weighing 42,000 lbs. would create a force of friction of 4200 lbs. The co-efficient of friction being but $\frac{1}{10}$th, if the diameter of the axle were 8 inches, and the number of revolutions 30 per minute, this resistance alone would equal 8-horse power.

Chapter VI. may be deferred until after reading that on the Resolution of Forces.

CHAPTER VI.

THE INCLINED PLANE.

The inclined plane is a smooth plane surface inclined at an angle to the horizon.

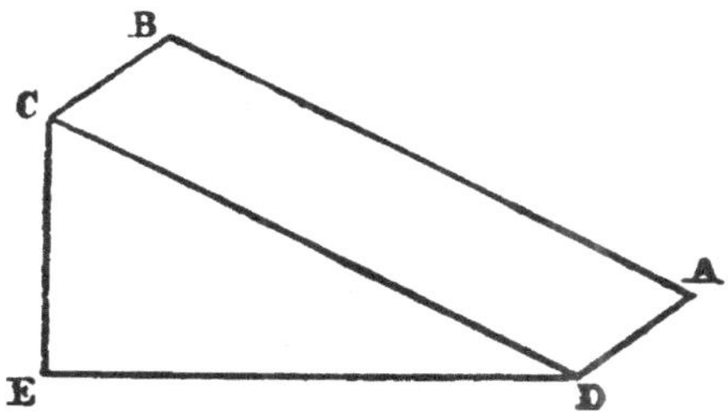

A B C D is an inclined plane.
A B is the length of the plane.
E C is the height of the plane.
D E is the base of the plane.
E D C is the angle of inclination.

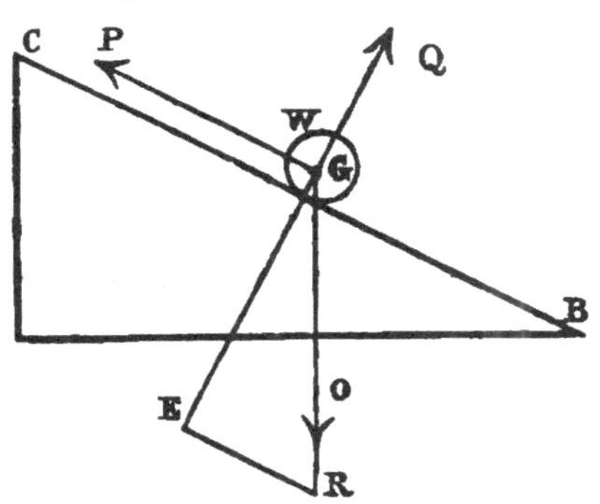

Let *us suppose* a weight, W, on an inclined plane,

and a force, P, acting parallel to the plane, there is equilibrium when—

The POWER *is to the* WEIGHT *as the vertical* HEIGHT *of the* PLANE *is to its* LENGTH :

$$P : W = H : L$$

The resistance of the plane acts in a direction perpendicular to its surface, as G Q. We may suppose the pressure on the plane replaced by a force applied in the direction G Q, and this force will represent the reaction of the plane, and if a force of sufficient magnitude be applied in the direction P, parallel to the plane, the plane may be removed, and the weight W will be supported.

The force G O may be resolved into two forces, G E and E R, now the force G E is balanced by the reaction of the plane, B C, which will balance any force perpendicular to B C, and the weight W will be kept in equilibrium if the force E R be counteracted by an equal and opposite force, P, acting in the direction G P.

If the force P be represented by the line R E, and the weight W by the line G R, there will be equilibrium, that is :

$$P : W = RE : GR$$

From the centre of gravity of the body, suppose a line drawn parallel to the plane, the direction of this line is the most useful application of the force.

When the power is applied parallel to the base of the plane, then—

The POWER *is to the* WEIGHT *as the vertical* HEIGHT *of the* PLANE *is to its* BASE :

$$P : W = H : B$$

A weight on one inclined plane is sometimes made

to raise a weight on another inclined plane; this is frequently employed on railroads, where a loaded waggon descends an incline and raises another waggon on the ther.

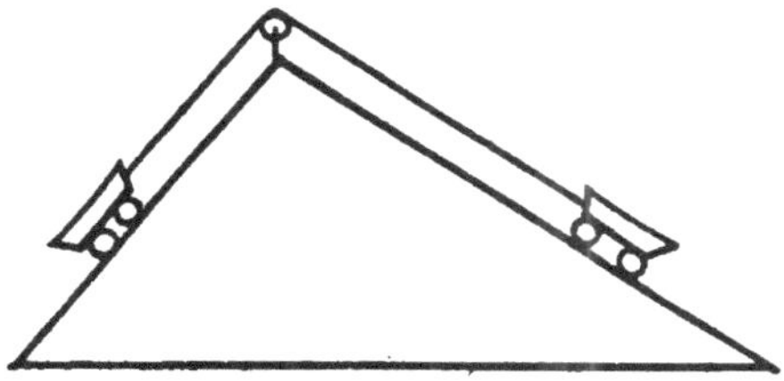

Some of the examples of inclined planes are to be found in the construction of common roads and railways. On the sides of the railway you may see a kind of finger-post, showing the inclination of the road: as 1 in 20, which means that if 20 yards or feet, or any other unit, be taken, the road rises or falls one yard or one foot in 20 feet or yards.

If it is required to find what force will be necessary to keep in equilibrium a railway waggon weighing 4 tons upon an inclined plane which rises 6 feet in 120 of its length, then, as the length 120 is to the height 6, so is 4 tons to the answer.

Examples.

1. What power would be necessary to support a weight of 4 lbs. on an inclined plane whose height is 5 inches and length 2 feet 6 inches?

$$P : W = \text{Height} : \text{Length}$$
$$P : 64 \text{ ozs.} = 5 \text{ in.} : 30 \text{ in.}$$
$$\therefore P = \frac{5 \times 64}{30} \text{ ozs.} = 10\tfrac{2}{3} \text{ ozs.}$$

The principle of virtual velocity mentioned under the lever may be applied the same as in every other mechanical power. The *power* multiplied by the space through which it moves is equal to the *weight* multiplied by the vertical space through which it ascends.

2. Suppose an inclined plane 30 feet long, and the vertical height 1 foot, the weight W 30 lbs., and the power 1 lb., it is obvious that to raise W vertically 2 feet, the power must descend a space of 30 feet.

3. A road rises 2 yards in 64; what power would be necessary to support a weight of 96 lbs.?

4. What power must a man exert who has to raise a hogshead weighing 964 lbs., upon an inclined plane 8 feet high and 36 feet long?

5. What is the length of an inclined plane when the vertical height is 3 feet, the weight of the body 56 lbs., and the power 16 lbs.?

6. What is the vertical height of an inclined plane when the length is 2 feet 6 inches, and a body weighing 96 lbs. is kept in equilibrium by a power of 20 lbs.?

7. What power will be necessary to keep a weight of 50 lbs. in equilibrium when the length of the plane is 6 feet and the height of the plane 1 foot 6 inches?

8. What weight will a power of 6 lbs. sustain on an inclined plane, when the vertical height of the plane is 5 feet and the length 90 feet?

9. The height of an inclined plane is 3 feet 6 inches, and its length 20 feet, what power would be required to raise 5 cwts.?

10. The length of an inclined plane is 32 feet, and a weight of 24 lbs. sustains 3 cwts.; what is the height of the plane?

11. On an inclined plane, whose base is 30 inches and length 40 inches, a weight of 3 lbs. is supported; what is the pressure on the plane?

12. What power will be required to support 56 lbs. on an inclined plane, whose height is 3 feet and length 8 feet?

13. An inclined plane rises 1 foot in 2 of its length; what weight would a power of 3 lbs. sustain?

14. What power must be applied to support a weight of 1 cwt. on an inclined plane, whose height is 30 inches and length 5 feet?

15. If a weight of 15 lbs. be placed on an inclined plane, whose base is 3 feet 6 inches and height 1 foot 9 inches, and the string by which it is supported be attached to an equal weight suspended over the top of the plane; how much must be added to the weight on the plane to produce equilibrium?

16. What power is required to roll a cask of sugar, weighing 926 lbs., into a door 5 feet high by means of a ladder 12 feet long?

17. If an inclined plane be 6 feet high, what is its length so that 5000 ozs. troy may be balanced on it by the same number of ounces avoirdupois weight?

18. If the length of an inclined plane is 90 feet and height 1 foot 6 inches, and the weight 30 cwts.; what power will be required to keep the body on the plane?

19. If the length of a plane is 15 feet and height 2 feet 6 inches, what is the ratio of the power to the weight?

20. The vertical height of a grocer's cart is 3 feet 6 inches; what power must be exerted to raise a cask of sugar weighing 16 cwts., by means of a plank 8 feet long?

21. Two inclined planes of the same height are placed together, height to height; their lengths are

2 feet and 16 inches respectively, and two weights connected with a cord passing over a pulley resting upon them balance each other; the cord is parallel to the plane, and the weight which rests on the longer plane is 42 lbs.; what is the other weight?

22. A brewer's dray is 3 feet from the ground, and a barrel of beer weighing 390 lbs. is to be rolled up on an incline plane 8 feet long; what power will be required?

23. An inclined plane is 18 inches long, and a power of 3 lbs. supports 56 lbs.; what is the height of the plane?

24. When the power moves through a space of 20 feet, and the power is to the weight as 3 to 12, how far does the weight ascend vertically?

25. If a man can draw a weight of 2 cwts.; what weight could he draw up an inclined plane whose length is 23 feet and vertical height 3 feet?

26. A weight of 90 lbs. is sustained on an inclined plane whose height is 3 feet and length 48 inches; what is the power?

27. On an inclined railway which rises 1 in 20, what power is required to draw a train weighing 30 tons, neglecting the resistance of friction?

28. If a waggon weighing 2 tons rests on an inclined plane which rises 1 in 20, what is the pressure on the road?

29. A cord passes over the summit of two inclined planes, whose heights coincide, and supports at its extremities a weight on each plane; show that the weights are proportional to the lengths of the planes.

30. What weight would be required to sustain a weight of 80 lbs. on a plane inclined at an angle of 40° to the horizon?

31. If a power of 3 ozs. supports a weight of

8 oz. on an inclined plane, what is the pressure on the plane?

32. What weight can 3 lbs. sustain on an inclined plane, whose height is 15 inches and length 1 foot 8 inches?

33. A weight of 150 lbs. is sustained on an inclined plane by a cord parallel to the plane; this cord is attached to the extremity of one of the equal arms of a straight horizontal lever; the weight attached to the other end of the lever is 50 lbs.; compare the height of the plane with the length.

On an inclined plane, the time of a body falling down the plane is to the time of falling freely down the vertical height of the plane, as the length of the plane is to its height.

Let L represent the length of the plane, and
H the vertical height of the plane.

Now the force which urges the body down the plane is equal to a force acting in an opposition direction, which would keep it at rest on the plane; but we have seen that this force F is to the weight of the body W as the height H is to the length L.

F : W = H : L and the force which produces motion on the plane is $= \frac{WH}{L}$

The accelerating force on an incline is directly as the force, and inversely as the quantity of matter. Therefore

The accelerating force on an inclined plane : to the accelerating force of a body falling freely

$$=\frac{\text{W H}}{\text{W L}}:\frac{\text{W}}{\text{W}}=\text{H}:\text{L}$$

The force which carries the body down the plane is uniform accelerating force; the velocity then acquired in a unit of time measures this force.

Let Lv be the velocity acquired in a unit of time by a body falling freely, Hv will be the velocity acquired in the same time by falling down the plane; and if I and t be the times of falling down the length L, and of falling vertically down the height H,

$$\text{L}:\text{H}=\tfrac{1}{2}\,\text{H}v\text{T}^2:\tfrac{1}{2}\,\text{L}vt^2$$
$$\text{L}^2:\text{H}^2=\text{I}^2:t^2$$
$$\text{or L}:\text{H}=\text{T}:t$$

The velocity acquired by falling down the plane is equal to the velocity acquired by falling freely down the vertical height of the plane.

The accelerating force on the plane : to the accelerating force of a body falling freely $=\text{H}:\text{L}$

Also $\text{S}=\tfrac{1}{2}\,vt$ as before v is velocity acquired falling freely down H.

$$\text{L}:\text{H}=\tfrac{1}{2}\,vt:\tfrac{1}{2}\,vt=v\text{T}:vt$$
$$\text{But H}:\text{L}=t:\text{T}$$
$$\therefore \text{I}:i=\text{V}:v$$

Whence V and v, the velocity acquired down the plane is equal to the velocity acquired by falling freely down the vertical height of the plane.

THE WEDGE.

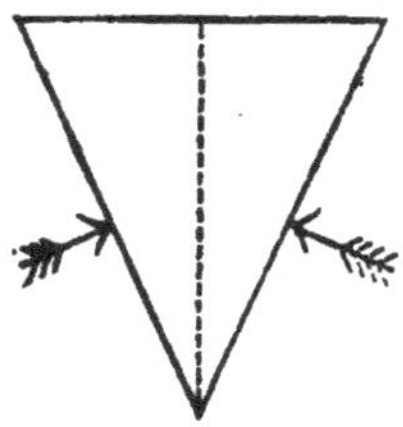

The wedge is commonly used for separating surfaces; it may be resolved into two inclined planes, joined base to base, but it is sometimes used as a single inclined plane, driven under props to buildings, and, when the base can rest on a horizontal surface, this is the proper shape of the wedge. For splitting timber the double wedge is generally used. The wedge is frequently called the moveable inclined plane, and is usually driven by the force of percussion. The proportion between a blow and a pressure cannot be well defined, so the theory for calculating the power of the wedge is of little practical value. The effective force of the wedge depends chiefly on the friction between its surfaces and the substances it is used to divide. The wedge is very useful where a great force has to be exerted through a small space. Masses of timber and stone are frequently split by a wedge; it is also employed to press oil out of seeds. Nails, razors, chisels, and plane-irons act on the principle of the wedge. The degree of inclination varies with the material they have to cut; tools for cutting wood the proper angle is about 30; those for cutting iron from 50 to 60, and those for cutting brass and copper from 80 to 90. The keystone of an arch acts on the principle of a wedge. When a wedge is driven into any body the friction on the sides is very great, and were it not for this friction the wedge would rebound every time it was struck. The only law that can be laid down with any certainty is *that the power is increased by diminishing the angle of the edge.*

THE SCREW.

If we take a piece of paper and cut it in the form of an inclined plane, and black the upper edge A C:

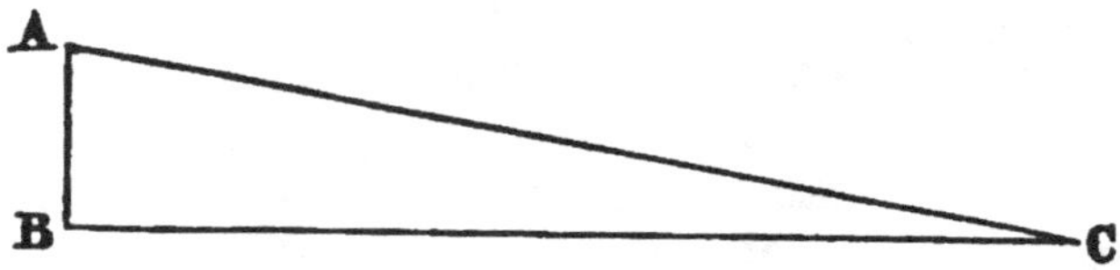

beginning with the end B C, wind it round a pencil or cylinder, the edge of the paper will represent the screw-line, or threads of the screw. ***A screw, then, is an inclined plane constructed on the surface of a cylinder.*** The distance between any two threads represents the perpendicular height of the inclined plane that extends once round the cylinder, which is usually stationary, and the screw moveable, but the nut may be moveable and the screw stationary.

In working the screw the power is frequently transmitted by causing the screw to move through the nut. The power is usually applied by means of a lever. We may deduce the working principle of the screw from that of the inclined plane when the power acts parallel to the base of the plane. The weight rests on the inclined face of the thread, and the power acts on the surface of a cylinder parallel to the base.

The power is to the resistance as the distance between two threads of the screw is to the circumference described by the point to which the power is applied.

P : R = distance between the threads : circumference described by the power

Examples.

1. The circumference of the circle described by a lever working a screw is 2 feet 9 inches, the space between the threads $\frac{1}{4}$ of an inch. If a force of 13 lbs. be applied to the lever, what will be the pressure of the screw?

2. The distance between the threads of a screw is $\frac{3}{4}$ of an inch; a lever 6 feet 6 inches long works the screw. What force must be applied to draw a weight of 150 tons up an inclined plane whose height is in the ratio of 2 to 12?

3. The distance between two threads of a screw is $\frac{1}{2}$ inch, and the circle described by the lever 60 inches. If a force of 1 lb. were applied to the lever what weight would it sustain?

4. In a screw 6 inches long there are 36 threads; the screw is worked with a windlass, the radius of which is 18 inches. What power must be exerted to raise a weight of 3 tons?

5. In a screw 9 inches long there are 27 threads, the screw is worked with a windlass, the radius of which is 2 feet; what power must be exerted to raise 2 tons 12 hundred-weight?

6. The distance between the threads of a screw is $\frac{3}{4}$ of an inch; the length of the lever 34 inches. What is the ratio of the power to the weight?

7. If the interval between two threads of a screw be $\frac{1}{8}$ of an inch, and the diameter of the circle described by the lever 60 inches, what power must be applied to raise a weight of three tons?

8. A screw with the threads $\frac{1}{2}$ inch apart is worked with a windlass which has a radius of 18 inches. The threads of the screw act on the cogs of a wheel whose diameter is to that of the axle as 6 to 2. Attached to

the axle is a weight of 2 tons suspended by a rope. What force must be exerted on the windlass to keep the weight in equilibrium?

9. A carriage weighing half a ton is raised by a screw-jack. The threads of the screw are $\frac{1}{6}$ of an inch apart, and the lever is 16 inches. What power is applied to work the lever?

10. A lever 24 inches is worked with a force of 60 lbs. The threads of the screw are $\frac{1}{8}$ inch apart. What pressure is exerted by the screw?

11. What force must be exerted on a lever 18 inches long, with the threads of the screw $\frac{1}{5}$ of an inch apart, so as to raise 3 tons?

12. What will be the pressure of a screw when a lever 2 feet 6 inches long is moved with a force of 50 lbs., and the threads of the screw $\frac{1}{2}$ inch apart?

13. If the distance between the threads of a screw is $\frac{3}{8}$ of an inch, and the power applied at the end of a lever 3 feet long, equals 90 lbs.; what will be the pressure of the screw?

14. If the threads of a screw are $\frac{1}{4}$ of an inch apart, and the length of the lever 9 feet 6 inches, moved with a force of 50 lbs.; what weight would the screw raise?

15. What is the ratio of the power to the resistance when the distance between the threads of the screw is 1 inch and the length of the lever 1 foot 7 inches?

16. The length of the lever working a screw is 48 inches, and is moved with a force of 1 lb. Suppose the threads to be $\frac{1}{2}$ inch apart; what weight would be raised?

17. The spiral distance between two threads of a screw is $\frac{1}{8}$ of an inch. A lever 8 inches long is moved with a force of 12 lbs. What is the power of the machine?

18. The lever working a screw is 2 feet 6 inches,

the distance between the threads $\frac{1}{8}$ of an inch. What force is required to produce a pressure of 8 tons?

19. The distance between the threads of a screw is $\frac{1}{3}$ of an inch. What weight can be raised by a power of 60 lbs. applied at the extremity of a lever 1 foot 3 inches long?

20. What must be the distance between the threads of a screw, so that a power of 28 lbs. applied at the extremity of a lever 25 inches long may sustain a weight of 10,000 lbs.?

21. The weight of a gun is 2016 lbs., the distance of the elevating screw and the centre of gravity of the gun from the axis are respectively 36 inches and 4 inches. If the distance between the threads of the screw be $\frac{2}{3}$ of an inch, and the length of the lever 5 inches, what power must be applied to keep the gun in a horizontal position?

22. The distance between the threads of a screw being $\frac{1}{2}$ inch, and the circumference described by the lever 10 feet; what is the ratio between the power and the weight?

23. If a power of 20 lbs. acting at the end of a lever attached to a screw describes a circle of 100 inches; what resistance will the power overcome the distance between the threads of the screw bend 1 inch?

CHAPTER VII.

COMPOSITION AND RESOLUTION OF FORCES.

If a body is struck in opposite directions by two equal forces, the body will remain at rest: but if the forces are unequal, then the body will move with a diminished force in the direction of the greater blow. But if a body be struck at the same instant by two forces in different directions, then the body will move in a line, lying in the same plane between the directions of the two forces. If these forces were equal, and struck the body at right angles, then it would move in the diagonal of a square.

Let X represent a ball struck by two equal forces at right angles to each other; suppose the force A to

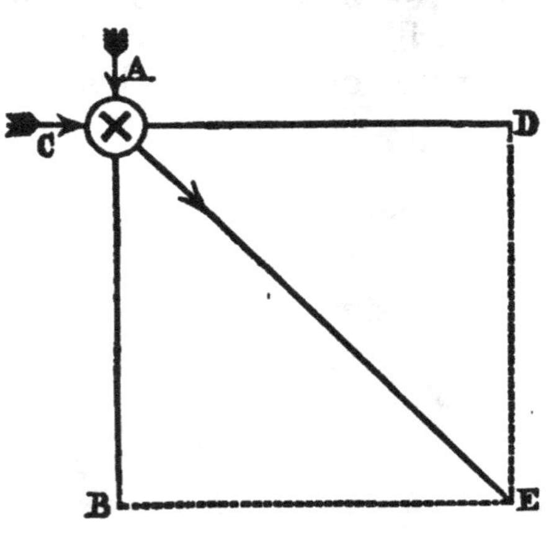

send it from X to B, and the force C to send it from X to D; then the ball will go in the direction X E, the diagonal of the square X B E D. This line represents the resultant of the two forces A and C, which are called its components.

The time the body takes to go from X to E is exactly the same as it would have taken to travel from X to B or X to D.

If two unequal forces—say one of 3, and the other 6—act at right angles to a body, it will move in the direction of the diagonal of a rectangle.

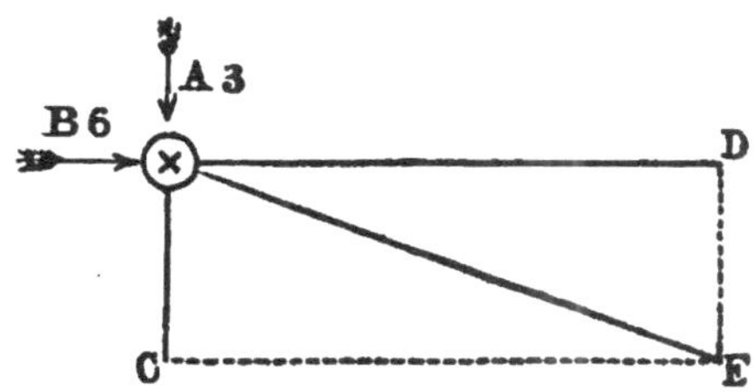

Let X be acted on by A=3 and B=6. The force A would send it to C, and the force B would send it twice as far to D; then the ball will not move in the direction of either force, but in the direction of X E, the diagonal of the rectangle X C E D.

When two forces act in the direction of an acute or obtuse angle, the body will move in the direction of the diagonal of a parallelogram.

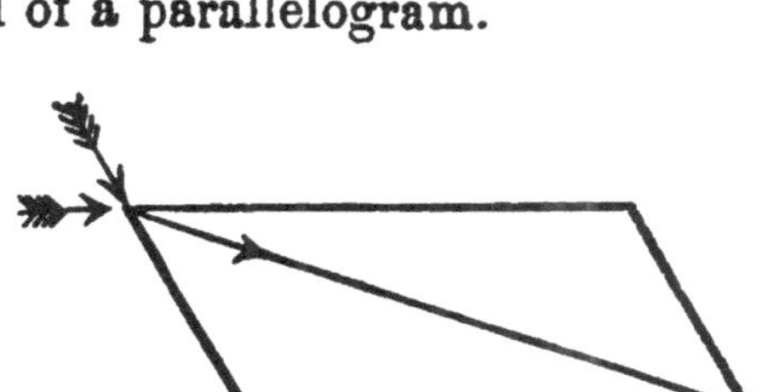

The resultant is, in fact, the compounded result of the two motions. Suppose two railway trains travelling at the same rate in the same direction, and a passenger were to throw across to his friend in the opposite carriage an apple, it would appear to go straight across; but this is not its direction, for in its course through the air it travels in the diagonal of a parallelogram, formed by the lines representing the direction in which the trains are travelling, and perpendicularly drawn from the points from which the one tosses and the other catches the apple.

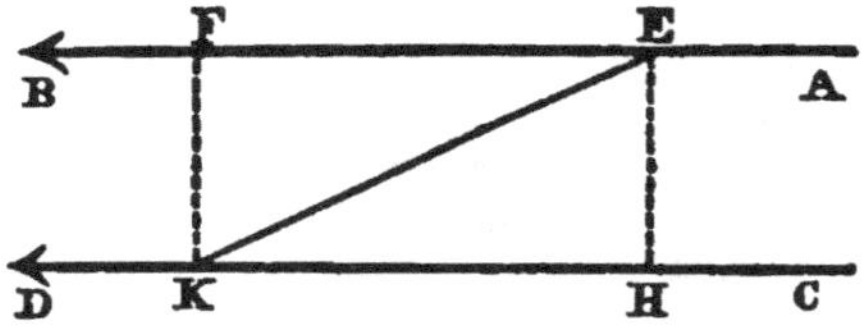

Let A B and C D represent the direction of the trains, E the point from whence the apple is thrown; while the apple is travelling across, the trains have passed from E and H to F and K. But the apple having the same motion as the train, which would have carried it from E to F, and a projectile force which would have carried it across to H, moves in the direction E K, the diagonal of a rectangle.

The parallelogram of forces has a variety of illustrations in practical life.

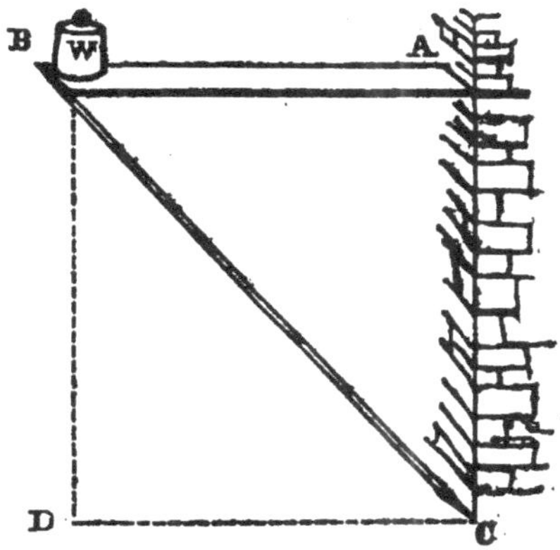

Let us suppose a piece of timber projecting from a wall, and loaded with a weight W, and let it be required to determine the strain on the timbers A B and B C, and upon the wall: complete the parallelogram A B, D C, and divide B D into as many equal parts as there are units of weight in W, and with the same scale of equal parts find how many such parts are contained in B A and B C.

The numbers obtained will equal the units of weight in A B and C B.

The point B is held at rest by forces in the direction B D, B A, and C B, and these are represented in magnitude and direction by the sides and diagonal of a parallelogram. C B represents the diagonal, and B D, B A represent the direction and magnitude of the other forces.

It is plain that no matter how many forces, or in what direction they act upon a body, it can only begin to move in one direction.

For instance, a boat may be moved by the force of the wind, the force of the tide, and by the oars. Now we can imagine a single force attached to the boat, and fastened in such a direction as would keep the boat at rest notwithstanding these forces; or we might suppose it acting in such a direction as to be equal to the forces of the wind, tide, and oars, and supply their place. This force would be the resultant of the three forces. When two forces act upon a point in different directions, the resultant is found geometrically. The line representing this force must lie in the same plane which contains the direction of the other forces.

If the adjacent sides of a parallelogram represent the component forces in direction and magnitude, the diagonal will represent the resultant force in direction and magnitude.

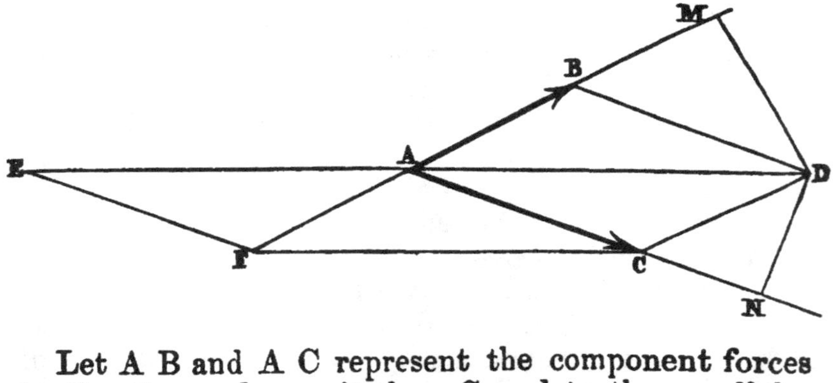

Let A B and A C represent the component forces in direction and magnitude. Complete the parallelogram, and draw the diagonal A D. A D will represent the resultant of A B, and A C in direction and magnitude. Produce A B and A C, and from D draw D M and D N perpendicular to A B and A C.

In the triangles D B M, D C N; the angle D M B = D N C being right angles, and angle D B M = angle B A C (because B D and A C are parallel, and M B A *cuts them*) = angle D C N, therefore the third angle

B D M of the one triangle equals the third angle C D N of the other, and the triangles are equiangular and similar:

∴ C D : D N = B D : D M, and alternately
C D : B D = D N : D M

Now we can imagine A D to be a lever whose fulcrum is at D, which is acted on by the forces A B, A C applied at the point A, and since the force in the line A M : to force in line A N :: A B : B C

= C D : B D, since B C is a parallelogram
= D N : D M

The two forces acting on the lever A D are inversely as the perpendiculars from the fulcrum on their lines of action, and therefore the lever will be kept in equilibrium about D. But the lever will also be kept at rest by the resultant of the forces, since the single force produces the same effect as they do when they act at the same point and at the same instant. The resultant, therefore, must act in the line A D, for it keeps the lever at rest, which it could not do if it acted at A, and made any angle with the lever A D on either side of it.

To show that the diagonal represents the force in magnitude:

Produce D A, and suppose a force A E to be taken equal to and opposite to the resultant of A B and A C. The joint effect of A B and A C will now be counteracted by A E, and the point which is acted on by the three forces, A B, A C, and A E, will remain at rest. Whatever, therefore, be the effect produced by the joint action of A E and A C, it is counteracted by A B; that is, A B must be equal and opposite to the resultant of A E and A C.

Complete the parallelogram E C, and draw the diagonal A F. Now A F is the line in which the resultant of A E and A C acts, and since the force A B is equal and opposite to that resultant, A F must be in the same straight line A B, and equal and parallel to C D. Wherefore F D is a parallelogram, and E C and F D being parallelograms, A E = F C = A D. The resultant, therefore, of A B and A C, which is equal and opposite to A E, will be represented in magnitude by A D, the diagonal of the parallelogram, of which A B and A C are the sides.

If three forces represented in magnitude and direction by the sides of a triangle taken in order act at a point, they will keep it in equilibrium.

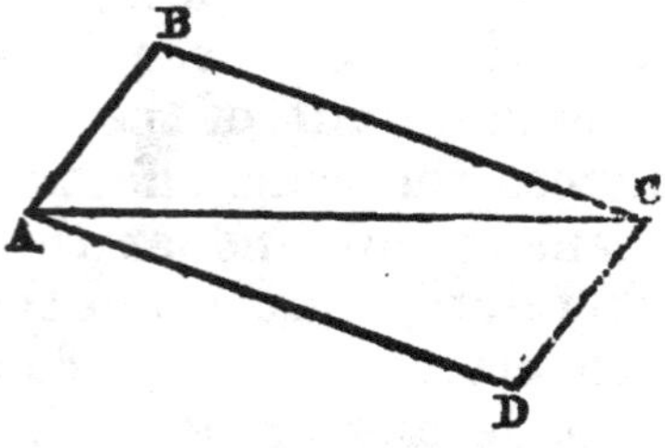

Let three forces, A B, B C, C A represented in magnitude and direction by the sides of the triangle A B C, taken in order, act on the point A; they will keep it in equilibrium. Complete the parallelogram A B C D; then the force represented by B C is also represented by A D, and acts on the point A; and the resultant of the forces A B, A D is represented in magnitude and direction by A C.

Therefore the forces A B, B C, C A produce the same effect as A C, C A; that is, they will keep the point A at rest.

If the sides of a polygon taken in order represent in

magnitude and direction forces which act simultaneously at a point, they will keep it at rest.

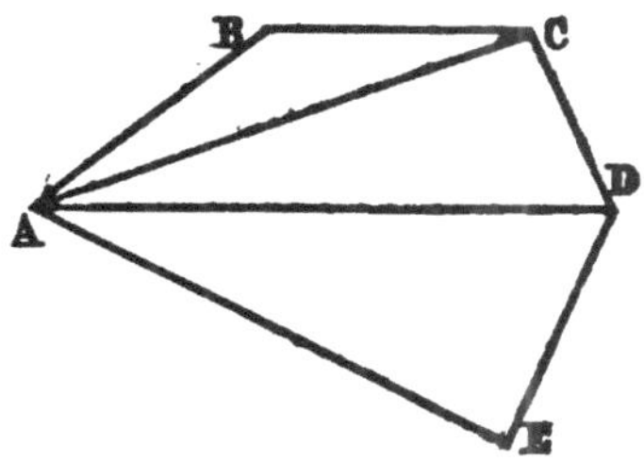

Let A B, B C, C D, D E, E A represent in magnitude and direction forces acting together at the point A, they will keep it in equilibrium.

The forces A B, B C are equivalent to a force A C.

Therefore, the forces A B, B C, C D are equivalent to the forces A C, C D, that is, to force A D.

Again, the forces A B, B C, C D, D E are equivalent to the forces A D, D E, that is, to force A E.

Therefore, finally, the forces A B, B C, C D, D E, E A are equivalent to forces A E, E A, but A E and E A are equal and opposite, and, therefore, will keep the point A in equilibrium.

Examples.

When forces act at right angles to each other, the resultant force is easily found.

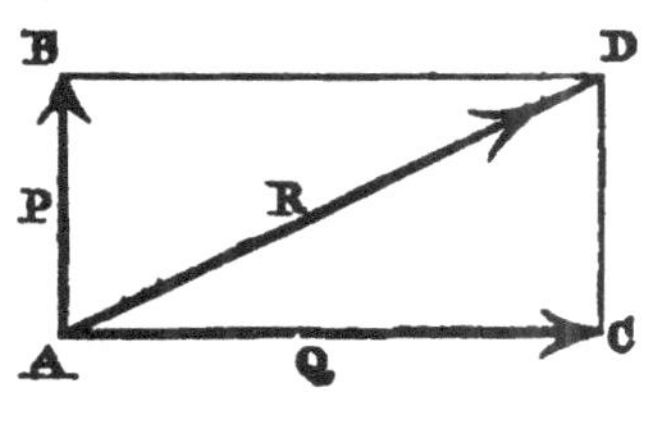

Let A B, A C represent in direction and magnitude

two forces acting at a point A, at right angles to each other. Complete the parallelogram, and join A D, then A D represents the resultant of A B and A C.

Now the square of A D = the squares on A B and B D = the squares on A B and A C.

Let A B, A C, and A D represent P, Q and R:

$$P^2+Q^2=R^2$$

From this any one of the three forces may be found if the other two are given.

1. Two forces of 6 and 8 act at right angles. What is their resultant?

$$R^2=P^2+Q^2=6^2+8^2=36+64=110$$
$$\therefore\ R=\sqrt{110}=10{\cdot}47$$

2. Two forces acting at right angles to each other produce a resultant of 20, one of the forces = 12. What is the other force?

3. Two forces in the ratio of 16 to 30 act at right angles to each other. What is the resultant force?

4. The resultant of two forces acting at right angles to each other is 35, one of the forces = 21. What is the other force?

5. Two forces of 16 and 64 act at right angles to each other. What is the resultant?

6. The resultant of two forces acting at right angles is 64, one of the forces = 28. What does the other force equal?

7. Two forces in the ratio of 3 : 6 act at right angles to each other, and produce a resultant of 30. What are the forces?

8. Two forces of 10 lbs. and 34 lbs. act at right angles upon a point. What is their resultant?

9. The resultant of two forces is 54, one of the *forces* = 32. Find the other force.

CHAPTER VIII.

FALLING BODIES.

A BODY falling through the atmosphere is subject to the operation of two forces, gravity and the resistance of the fluid through which it falls. The weight of the body alone, under the constant action of gravity, would produce a constantly accelerated velocity, but the resistance of the air increases with the velocity, and sometimes (though not often) becomes equal to the weight of the body, in which case the forces are balanced and the body is in equilibrium. The descent of a parachute when detached from a balloon is subject to the constant force of gravity, and falls with an increasing velocity, till the resistance of the air becomes equal to its weight. The force of gravity is then balanced by the resisting medium through which the body falls, and its velocity, instead of being accelerated, is uniform.

We have seen that all bodies tend to fall with the same velocity, and that this velocity is a continually increasing one.

The attraction of the earth never ceases to act, and the body is constantly receiving a new impulse at every instant of its fall, each giving it an increased velocity, so that the final velocity may be regarded as the sum of the equal increments of velocity thus communicated by the force of the earth's attraction.

From experiments made by Atwood's machine, the law of falling bodies has been fully established. Let us suppose a body to fall from the top of a very high tower; it starts from a state of rest, and in the first second falls through a space of 16 feet,* and has acquired a velocity of 32 feet. The velocity of the body at the end of the first second would carry it through 32 feet in the second second, if the velocity were uniform; but it is constantly accelerated in its descent, and at the end of the second second it has acquired a velocity of twice 32, or 64 feet; at the end of the third second it has acquired a velocity of three times 32, or 96 feet per second, and so on.

The space through which the body falls in each second taken separately will be as the odd numbers:

1, 3, 5, 7, 9, &c.

The body falls during	the	1st	second,	$1\times16=\ \ 16$	feet
,,	,,	2nd	,,	$3\times16=\ \ 48$	,,
,,	,,	3rd	,,	$5\times16=\ \ 80$	,,
,,	,,	4th	,,	$7\times16=112$	,,
,,	,,	5th	,,	$9\times16=144$	,,

The whole space through which a body has fallen is determined by squaring the number of seconds occupied by the fall, and multiplying the product by 16, *the space through which the body falls in one second.*

Space fallen through	in	1 sec.		$=\ 1\times16$
,,	,,	2 secs.	$2\times2=$	$4\times16=\ \ 64$ ft.
,,	,,	3 ,,	$3\times3=$	$9\times16=144$ ft.
,,	,,	4 ,,	$4\times4=$	$16\times16=256$ ft.
,,	,,	5 ,,	$5\times5=$	$25\times16=400$ ft.

* This is only an approximation. The actual distance is $16\frac{1}{12}$, or 16 feet one inch. I have omitted the fractions to simplify the *operations.*

The same rule applies to any number of seconds, or fractional parts of seconds.

We have considered these laws with special reference to falling bodies, but they apply to every uniformly accelerated motion, such as the rolling of a ball down an inclined plane, and the ascent of light bodies through water. In such cases, while the rule remains the same as for falling bodies, allowance must be made for the resistance and friction to which the body is subjected, and the numerical results of the calculations will vary in each case.

Ascent of Bodies.

As all bodies are uniformly accelerated in their descent, they are uniformly retarded in their ascent. The velocity of a falling body increases with equal additions in equal times; in the ascent of body it is retarded by equal losses in equal times. In fact, all the phenomena attending the accelerated descent of falling bodies is exhibited in a reversed order when a body is projected upwards. A body thrown upwards and left to the action of gravity, rises during any second 32 feet less than it did in the previous second, until its velocity is reduced to 0, when it descends like any other falling body, gaining 32 feet of downward motion every second, which is the same as it lost in its upward motion, so that its ascent and descent will occupy the same time.

Let us suppose a body to begin its ascent with a velocity of $160=10\times16$ feet. The body will move according to the following table:

In the 1st sec. it rises		$10 \times 16 - 1 \times 16 = 9 \times 16 = 144$ ft.
„	2nd	„	$10 \times 16 - 3 \times 16 = 7 \times 16 = 112$ ft.
„	3rd	„	$10 \times 16 - 5 \times 16 = 5 \times 16 = 80$ ft.
„	4th	„	$10 \times 16 - 7 \times 16 = 3 \times 16 = 48$ ft.
„	5th	„	$10 \times 16 - 9 \times 16 = 1 \times 16 = 16$ ft.

At the commencement of the 6th second the body commences its descent. Its final velocity is equal to its initial velocity, and at any point in its course the velocity, either ascending or descending, is equal.

Projection of Bodies Horizontally.

When a body is thrown vertically upwards, or downwards, it will move in a vertical line, because the force of projection and that of gravity act in the same line.

A body thrown in a horizontal direction, or at any angle with the horizon, describes in its course a curved line called a parabola. The instant a body is thrown into space it is acted on by three forces: the force of gravity, which is always the same; the resistance of the air; and the force of projection.

Let us suppose a cannon-ball thrown from the top of a tower in a horizontal direction; and let us further suppose the height of the tower such that the ball would have fallen by its gravity to the ground in three seconds. The ball projected horizontally, no matter what the force may be, will reach the ground in the same time as if it had fallen by its own gravity from the top of the tower. From this it appears that horizontal motion does not interfere with the action *of gravity*, but that a projectile descends with the same rapidity when moving forwards as if it were only acted upon by the force of gravity.

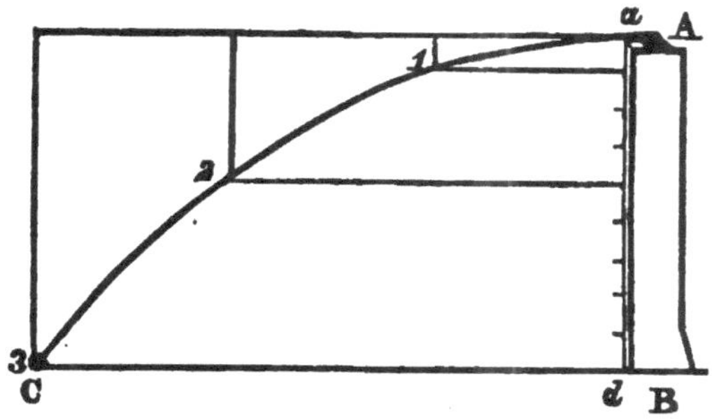

Let A B be the vertical height of the tower, and the path of the projectile *a* C.

During the first second the ball is at 1.

During the second second it is at 2.

During the third second it is at 3.

The same as if it had fallen from *a* to *d*, the perpendicular height of the tower.

A rifleman in firing at a fixed object makes a little allowance for the descent of the ball by gravity, and aims a little above the point he is anxious to strike. A sight is placed on guns and rifles for this purpose.

Examples.

We have seen that when a body falls freely by the action of gravity for one second, it acquires at the end of that time a velocity of 32 feet. The velocity V then equals gravity G, multiplied by the time T.

$$V = G\,T$$

1. To find the velocity (V) acquired by a body which falls for 20 seconds:

$$V = G\,T = 32 \times 20 = 640 \text{ feet per second}$$

2. To find the space (S) fallen through in the same time:

$$S = \frac{1}{2} G T^2 = 16 \times 20^2 = 6400 \text{ feet}$$

3. To find in what time a body falls through 1024 feet:

$$1024 = 16 \times T^2,\ T^2 = 64,\ T = 8$$

4. To find the velocity (V) acquired in the same space:

$$V = G T = 32 \times 8 = 256 \text{ feet per second}$$

5. A body is thrown directly upwards, with a velocity of 1000 feet per second. How high will it ascend?

Now the height to which it will ascend is the same as that through which it must fall to acquire the same velocity:

$$\text{Since } V = G T,\ 1000 = 32\,T,\ T = \frac{1000}{32} = \frac{125}{4} = 31\tfrac{1}{4}$$

$$S = \frac{1}{2} G T^2 = 16 \frac{(125)^2}{(4)^2} = (125)^2 = 15625 \text{ feet}$$

To find the space through which a body falls in a given time, square the number of seconds occupied by the fall, and multiply the product by 16 *the space through which the stone falls in one second:*

$$S = \frac{1}{2} G T^2 = 16 \times 6^2 = 576 \text{ feet}$$

Exercises.

1. A body is observed to occupy 5 seconds in its fall. Through what space has it fallen?

2. The light of a meteor is seen bursting in the air, and in 29 seconds afterwards a meteoric stone reaches the ground. Supposing the stone to have fallen perpendicularly; how far was the meteor from the earth?

3. A boy raised his kite with a small wooden figure of a man attached to the tail. The string by which it was attached broke, and the figure occupied 7 seconds in falling to the ground. What height was the kite?

4. A body has been falling 3 seconds. What is its velocity?

5. Through what space does a body fall during the 6th second of its descent?

6. Suppose a stone is 4 seconds in reaching the surface of the water in a well, what is the depth of the well, neglecting the rate at which sound travels?

7. What is the space described in the 7th second by a falling body?

8. What is the space described by a falling body during the 5th second?

9. What is the height of a tower from the water, supposing a stone to occupy 3 seconds in its fall?

10. Find the space through which a body would fall during the 13th second?

11. A boy dropped a stone from the top of a rock, the stone was 4 seconds falling to the earth. What was the height of the tree?

12. If a ball fall from the top of a bastion, and reaches the ground in 3 seconds, what is its height?

13. Through what space would a body fall in 2 seconds by the action of gravity?

14. A stone let fall from a balloon was 6 seconds reaching the earth. How high was the balloon?

15. What is the velocity of a falling body in $\frac{9}{16}$ seconds?

Now the velocity acquired in one second is the measure of the earth's gravity. We have seen that this velocity is 32.

Multiply 32 *by the number of seconds the body is falling, and the product will be the velocity.*

$$V = G\ T = 32 \times 9 = 288$$

The velocity divided by the measure of earth's gravity 32 *will give the time.*

A body falls with a velocity of 288 *feet. How long has it been falling?*

$$\frac{V}{G} = T = \frac{288}{32} = 9$$

16. How long will a body be falling 316 feet?

17. A body falls with a velocity of 290 feet. How long has it been falling?

18. What is the velocity of a body in 7 seconds?

19. How long will a body be falling 224 feet?

20. From what height must a body fall to acquire a velocity of 256 feet?

21. What is the velocity of a falling body in 9 seconds?

22. A body fell to the earth with a velocity 14 feet; from what height did it fall?

23. How long must a body fall to acquire a velocity of 200 feet?

24. A stone fell to the earth from a balloon with a velocity of 1240 feet. How high was the balloon?

25. If a stone be dropped from a balloon a quarter of a mile high; how long would it be reaching the earth, and what would be its final velocity?

26. If a stone be $2\frac{1}{2}$ seconds falling from the top of a spire to the earth; what is the height of the spire?

27. If a body be thrown upwards with an initial velocity of 125 feet per second; to what height will it ascend, and what will be its height and velocity at the end of 2 seconds?

28. If a stone dropped from the top of a rock be $3\frac{1}{2}$ seconds reaching the water; what is the height of the rock above the water, neglecting the rate at which sound travels?

29. Suppose a body to ascend with an initial velocity of 160 feet in a second; how long would it continue to ascend, and to what height would it go?

Divide the initial velocity in one second by 32, *and the quotient will be the time in seconds.*

Square the time and multiply by 16, *and the product will be the height in feet.*

Initial velocity 160 feet divided by $32 = 5$ seconds.

Time squared $5 \times 5 = 25 \times 16 = 400$ feet, the height to which the body ascended.

The answers, then, are 5 seconds and 400 feet.

30. A bullet is shot vertically upwards, and returned to the ground in 16 seconds. How high did it ascend?

31. How high will a stone rise which is thrown by a boy with a force sufficient to carry it 48 feet in the first second?

32. A rocket begins to ascend with a velocity of 176 feet in a second. How high will it ascend, and what time will be occupied in its ascent and descent?

CHAPTER IX.

MOMENTUM.

A STONE thrown by the hand, or a bullet projected by gunpowder, describes a path in space in obedience to the force which has acted upon it. If the stone or bullet met with no resistance from the air or any solid body—in other words, if no other force acted upon it —it would continue to move with the same velocity in the same direction for ever. The leaden bullet, moving through space, retains undiminished the force which has been impressed upon it.

The same force which projects a bullet would scarcely move a cannon-ball. The common explanation of this would be, that the cannon-ball is so much heavier than the bullet. This is not the true explanation, for if the weight of the bodies be neutralised by being suspended, and both set in motion by the same force, they would not move with the same velocity.

Let us suppose a number of leaden bullets, whose masses were represented by the numbers 1, 2, 3, 4, 5, 6, &c.; and let us further suppose them projected by the explosion of the same weight of gunpowder, these bullets would move with the velocities of 1, $\frac{1}{2}$, $\frac{1}{3}$, $\frac{1}{4}$, $\frac{1}{5}$, $\frac{1}{6}$, &c., so that the bullet whose mass was 6 would acquire from the same force a velocity of $\frac{1}{6}$; and a mass represented by 100, would have a velocity 100 times less than the mass represented as 1.

From this we learn, *that when the same force acts upon bodies free to move, their velocities are in the inverse ratio of their masses.*

The mass of a moving body multiplied by its velocity, gives the momentum, or quantity of motion.

The *momentum* of a body must not be confused, as is sometimes the case, with the *moving force.*

The *moving force* is the *momentum generated in one second*; that is, *moving force* is the product of the *mass* and the velocity acquired in 1 second.

When we come to speak of what is called *accelerating* force, the pupil will more fully comprehend the distinction. It is a common mistake to confound the terms, and therefore it was necessary to point it out.

In comparing the momenta of bodies, the velocities, the spaces, and weights, must be respectively of the same denomination.

Examples.

A bullet weighing $1\frac{1}{2}$ oz. is shot from a rifle with a velocity of 1100 yards in a second; and a ball weighing $2\frac{1}{2}$ lbs. is shot from a cannon with a velocity 900 feet in a second, which body has the greater momentum?

Let the *mass* of $\frac{1}{2}$ oz. be the *unit* of mass here; and let 1 foot and 1 second be that of space and time respectively;

Then, mass of the rifle-bullet $= 3$
and velocity (since 1100 yards $= 3300$ feet) $= 3300$
Also, mass of the ball (since $2\frac{1}{2}$ lbs. $= 80$ half-ounces) $= 80$
and velocity $= 900$
Hence, the momentum of the rifle-bullet $= 3 \times 3300 = 9900$
and momentum of the ball $= 80 \times 900 = 72{,}000$.

In the following examples, take 1 second, 1 foot, 1 lb. as the units of time, space, and weight; and the *mass* of 1 lb. as the unit of *mass*.

1. What is the momentum of a body weighing 8 oz. moving with a velocity of 60 feet per second?

2. A steam-engine moves with a velocity 20 miles an hour, and weighs 6 tons, what is its momentum?

3. With what force would a wall be struck by a 60 lb. cannon-ball moving at the rate of 70 feet per second?

4. A body, whose weight is 15, has a velocity of 12, what is its momentum?

5. With what momentum does a bullet weighing half an ounce, and moving with a velocity of 80 feet per second, strike the target?

6. What is the momentum of a body with a velocity of 15 and a weight of 60?

7. With what force would a steam-engine weighing 8 tons, and moving with a velocity of 30 miles an hour, strike any opposing fixed object?

8. The weight of a body is 19, its velocity 60, what is its momentum?

9. The weight of a body is 60, and its velocity 19, what is its momentum?

10. A stone weighing 16 oz. moves with a velocity of 36 feet per second, with what force will it strike any opposing object?

We have seen in the above examples that the momentum of a body is the product of the mass and velocity.

To obtain the velocity:

Divide the momentum by the mass and the quotient will be the velocity.

To obtain the weight:

Divide the momentum by the velocity and the quotient will be the mass, from which the weight is at once known.

11. The momentum of a body is 240, and its weight 6, what is its velocity?

$$\frac{240}{6} = 40 \text{ velocity.}$$

12. The momentum of a body is 68, and its velocity 4, what is the weight?

$$\frac{68}{4} = 17 \text{ mass, and } \therefore \text{ weight} = 17\text{lbs.}$$

according to our standard or unit.

13. The momentum of a steam-engine is 960, its velocity 25, required its weight?

14. The momentum of a stone is 260, its weight 12, what is its velocity?

15. A cannon-ball moves at the rate of 1000 feet a second, and has a momentum of 2750, what is its weight?

16. The momentum of a body is 690, the weight 23, what is the velocity?

When two bodies moving in opposite directions come into collision, they each lose an equal quantity of their momenta.

We have seen in the previous examples that momentum means the force necessary to destroy motion. Let us now consider what would be the effect of bodies coming into collision by moving in opposite directions. Suppose two bodies, equal in weight, moving with equal velocities in opposite directions, come into contact, one would destroy the force of the other, and *both bodies after* impact would be brought to a state of rest, for equal masses having the same velocities must produce equal forces.

Again: suppose one of the bodies to be double the weight or mass of the other, and by moving in opposite directions with equal velocities come in contact. Let us suppose the momentum (weight multiplied by velocity) of A to be $4 \times 12 = 48$, while that of B, which is double the weight, equals $8 \times 12 = 96$, after impact, 48 parts of motion in B will destroy 48 parts of motion in A, leaving only 48 parts in both bodies. Now the combined mass of both bodies is 12, and their momentum after impact 48, their velocity will be 48 divided by 12, which equals 4, so that they will move together with a velocity of 4, or $\frac{1}{12}$ of their velocity, before impact.

Two bodies may be unequal in mass and velocity. If the mass of a body, A, be 12, and its velocity 96, its quantity of motion or momentum will be $12 \times 96 = 1152$. If the mass of a body, B, be 9, and its velocity 25, its momentum will be $25 \times 9 = 225$. The sum of the two momenta or motions will be $225 + 1152 = 1377$, and this will be the whole motion or momentum of the united masses after collision, dividing 1377 by 21, the sum of $9 + 12$, the united masses of the bodies $= 65\frac{4}{7}$, the common velocity of the united masses after impact.

Two bodies moving in the same direction with different velocities, one may overtake and strike the other; the common velocity after impact may be determined by multiplying the number expressing the two masses by the number expressing the velocities. The sum of the two products so obtained, divided by the sum of the numbers expressing the two masses, will give a quotient, which will express the required *velocity*. *For* example: a body, A, weighs 9, moves with a velocity of 12; its quantity of motion is 108. A body, B, has a weight of 8, and moves with a velocity of 10; its momentum is therefore 80. The quantity of the two motions is $108+80=188$. This will be the whole motion of the united masses after impact. Divide 188 by the united weights $9+8=\frac{188}{17}=11\frac{1}{17}$ the quotient is $11\frac{1}{17}$, the velocity of the united masses after impact.

17. A body weighing 90 lbs. with a velocity 268, meets another coming in an opposite direction with a velocity of 20 and a weight of 10. What will be the result?

18. Required, the velocity of a cannon-ball weighing 68 lbs. to be equally effective with a battering-ram weighing 10,500 pounds, and propelled with a velocity of 18 feet in a second.

19. Let us suppose a comet, whose mass is represented by 1 and its velocity by 38; and let us further suppose the mass of the earth to be represented by 120 and its velocity by 12. With what force would these bodies, moving in opposite directions, strike each other, and what would be the result of the collision?

20. Two bodies, A and B, meet in opposite directions. The mass of A is 12 and its velocity 26. The velocity of B is 16 and its mass 19. What will be the result of the collision?

21. A boy, whose weight is 72 pounds, is running with a velocity of 6, and strikes another boy who is standing still, and whose weight is 96 pounds. What will be the result, supposing the boy who is standing still makes no resistance beyond his mere weight?

22. A cannon-ball, weighing 64 pounds, is moving on a smooth horizontal plane with a velocity of 25 feet a second, another ball is moving in an opposite direc-

tion with a velocity of 8 feet a second. What must be its weight to stop the motion of the cannon-ball?

23. Two boats, A and B, come into collision. The boat A is moving with a velocity 20 feet a second, and its weight is represented by 14 cwts. The boat B is moving with a velocity of 16 feet a second, and its weight is 12 cwts. What will be the result of the collision?

24. In a boat-race two boats, A and B, are rowing in the same direction. The boat A and its crew weigh 13 cwts. 6 lbs., and is moving with a velocity of 1 mile in 4 minutes. The boat B and its crew weigh $14\frac{1}{4}$ cwts., and is moving with the velocity of 28 feet a second. The swifter boat overtakes and strikes the other. What is the common velocity of both boats immediately after the blow?

25. Show the quantities of motion (or momenta) of two bodies, one of which is 35 times heavier than the other, but the smaller body moves 1500 times faster than the heavier body.

26. A body weighing 5 lbs., moving with a velocity of 25 feet a second, overtakes and strikes another body, weight $1\frac{1}{2}$ lbs., going in the same direction at the rate of 10 feet a second. What is their common velocity after collision?

CHAPTER X.

SOUND.

SOUND passes through the air at the rate of 1120 feet a second, and this applies to all sound whether loud or soft. The velocity of sound has sometimes been estimated a little more, but the state of the air must be taken into account. The higher the temperature the greater the velocity; this increase of velocity is about one foot for every degree the thermometer rises. But the experiments of Arago, Gay Lussac, and others, give 1120 when the thermometer stood at 61°.

Examples.

1. A flash of lightning was followed in 5 seconds by a clap of thunder. What was the distance of the cloud?

$$1120 \times 5 = 5600 \text{ feet}$$

2. A stone falls into a well, and after 3 seconds the splash is heard. How far from the top is the surface of the water?

3. A rocket explodes, and in 3 seconds the report of the explosion is heard. What is the distance of the rocket?

4. Standing on a hill I saw a woodman strike a tree with his axe, in 3½ seconds afterwards I heard the report. How far off was the woodman?

THE PENDULUM.

We have seen in Chapter VI. that a body descending down an inclined plane, or a succession of inclined planes, as A B, B C, C D, acquires the same velocity as if it had fallen the vertical height of the plane A E.

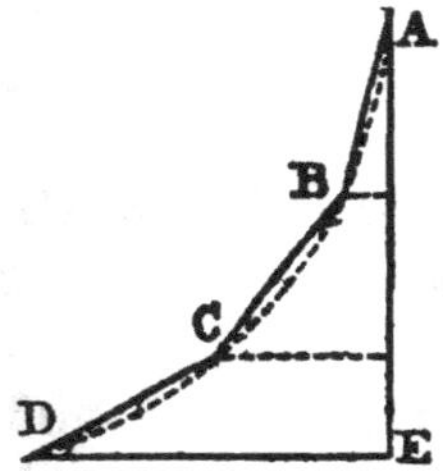

Now, the arc of a circle may be regarded as a succession of inclined planes, indefinitely small in length, and therefore a pendulum P in falling from D to C will acquire the same velocity as if it had fallen from B to C.

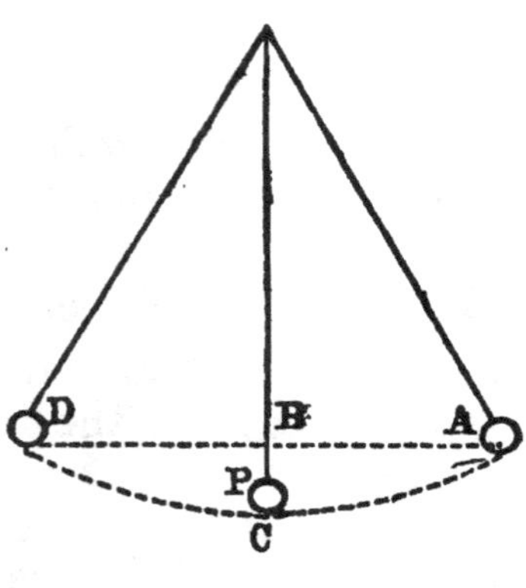

If the pendulum be raised to D and then released it will fall by its own gravity until it arrives at the vertical position C, whence the inertia will carry it almost to A, which is in a horizontal line with the point from which it descended. This has rendered the pendulum a valuable measurer of time.

Were it not for the resistance of the air and friction, it would ascend exactly to the point A. When it arrives at A its motion is spent, and gravity again acts upon it, carrying it up the opposite side of the arc. Gravity causes the pendulum to fall, and the force which it acquires in falling carries it up the opposite side of the arc. These motions of the pendulum are called its vibrations, or oscillations. The length of the arc in which the pendulum oscillates is called the amplitude of the arc. The vibrations of pendulums of equal lengths are nearly equal, whether the arc be great or small; that is, a pendulum will pass between the extremities of its arc always in the same time. If the pendulum fall from A it will go to B in the same time in which it would have gone

from C to D or from E to F. This is called the isochronism (equal-timed) of the pendulum, and this is entirely irrespective of the weight attached to the rod.

This equality of vibration, whether the arc be great or small, was a discovery of Galileo's.

The length of a pendulum, which vibrates sixty times in a minute, is about 39 inches. The longer a pendulum is the more slowly it vibrates, and the shorter it is the more quickly it vibrates; clocks are regulated by lengthening or shortening the pendulum. The oscillations of the pendulum being dependent on the force of gravity, the greater the force of gravity the more quickly will a pendulum vibrate. As the equatorial diameter of the earth exceeds the polar diameter, the poles of the earth must be nearer the centre of the earth's attraction than the equator, and the force of gravity at the poles must be greater because it is nearer the earth's centre. From this it will be seen that the length of a pendulum to vibrate in any given time must vary with the latitude of the place. The length of the pendulum is the distance from the point of suspension to a point called the centre of oscillation.

THE ELEMENTS OF HYDROSTATICS.

CHAPTER I.

Hydrostatics treat of fluids at rest, and hydrodynamics of fluids in motion. The following observations apply to fluids in a state of rest, except in the case of one or two machines:

A fluid is a material body composed of particles free to move in any direction by any force, however small.

Fluids have been divided into two classes, elastic and non-elastic.

Elastic fluids are those which are diminished in bulk by the application of pressure, such as air, gas, and steam;

Non-elastic fluids are those whose bulk cannot be altered by pressure except in the smallest degree, such as water and mercury.

Fluids and liquids are not the same. All liquids are fluids, but all fluids are not liquids. Air and gas are fluids, but not liquids. Water is a liquid and also a fluid.

The definition sometimes given of a liquid is any fluid that can be poured from one vessel to another.

There is one characteristic property by which these bodies are distinguished from solids. It is this: If we take a solid body and apply any pressure, that pressure is transmitted in the line of direction in which the force is applied; but if we apply pressure at any point of a fluid, this pressure is communicated equally in every direction.

As this principle is the very foundation of the science of hydrostatics, its meaning should be thoroughly comprehended, and progress is then comparatively easy.

If we take a leather bag and fill it with water, and apply pressure at any point, and then make holes in different parts of the bag with a pin, we should find the water spirt out with the same force, no matter at what points these holes were made.

If the particles of a fluid were arranged in regular columns — thus:  — there would be no lateral pressure, because one particle being in the same vertical line with those above it, the pressure could only be exerted perpendicularly downwards; but if the particles be arranged thus,  where one particle presses between two others, then there must be a lateral pressure, and were it not for this lateral pressure no water would issue from an aperture made in the side of a vessel. The upward pressure of water may be shown experimentally by taking a

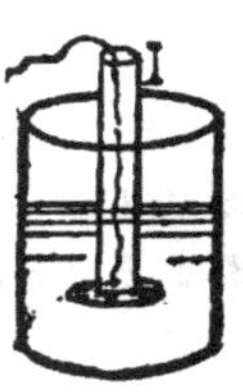

glass tube open at both ends. Let one of the ends of the tube be ground so as to fit a piece of slate; let the slate be held close to the bottom of the glass-tube by means of a string passing up the interior of the tube; the whole can now be immersed in water, and if the slate fits so as to prevent the water from entering the tube, the string may be dropped, and the slate will still remain at the bottom of the tube supported by the upward pressure of the water. By a similar experiment the upward pressure of the atmosphere may be illustrated. Fill a wine-glass with water, and cover it with a piece of writing-paper; press the paper firmly in contact with the top of the glass, so as to exclude all air between the surface of the water and the paper, then if the glass be inverted, and the hand removed, it will be found that the water will not fall out.

Fluids, then, press equally in all directions.

Let a close vessel of any shape be filled with a fluid, and let A B C D be similar, and equal portions taken out of the sides of the vessel, and these openings supplied with plugs fitting exactly and acted upon by pressures just sufficient to keep them at rest.

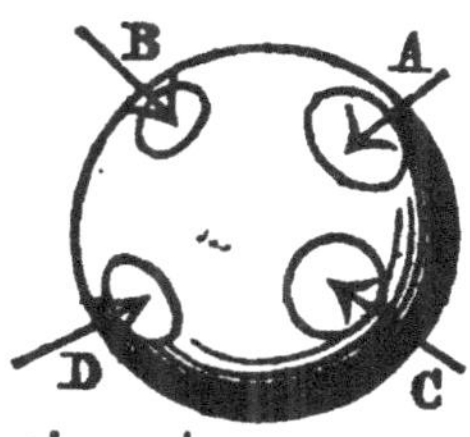

If an additional pressure be applied to any one of these plugs, all the others will move out unless an equal additional force be applied to them. This proves that the pressure communicated to one plug is transmitted by the fluid undiminished and unimpaired in every direction.

The pressure on any particle of a fluid of uniform density is proportional to its depth below the surface of the fluid.

Let the vertical lines P A, Q B be drawn from P and Q to the surface of the fluid. P and Q are two particles in a fluid of uniform density.

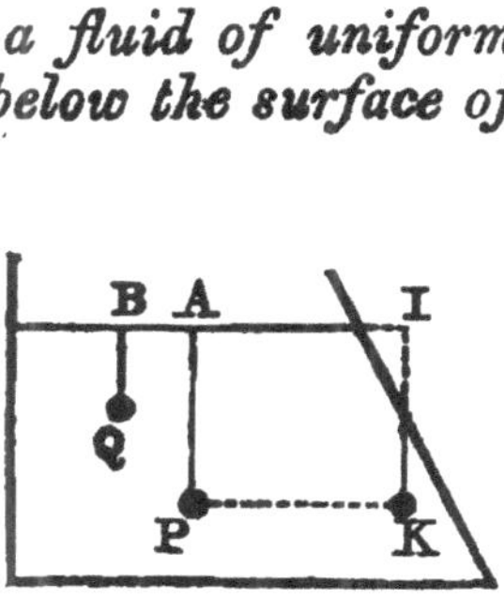

The pressure on the particle at P = weight of particles along the line P A, but as the density is uniform, every particle is of the same weight, and the weights of such lines of particles as P A, Q B will be proportional to their lengths.

∴ Pressure of particle at P : pressure on particle at Q = weight of the line P A of particles : to weight of the line Q B of particles :

= P A : Q B

It is found by experiment that whether a line of fluid particles extends vertically to the surface, as P A and Q B, or a portion of such line of particles is cut off by the side of the vessel, as at K, the pressure on K is the same as if the line of particles were continuous to K I, that is, wherever the particle is situated the pressure on it is proportional to its depth below the surface of the fluid.

When a fluid is at rest its surface is horizontal.

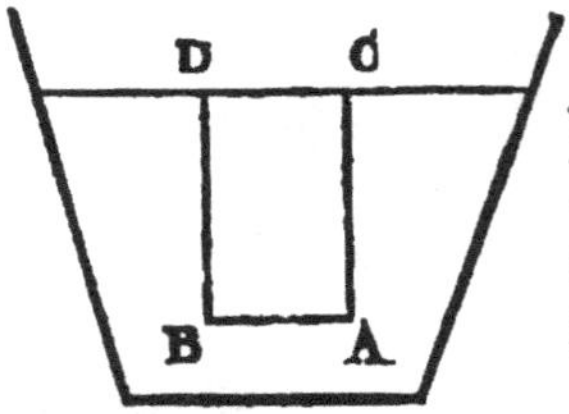

Let B A be a horizontal line in the interior of a fluid at rest, and B D and A C be vertical lines drawn from B A, meeting the surface of the fluid in D C.

Since the action of gravity on two particles, which we suppose situated at B and A, is perpendicular to the horizontal plane in which they lie, its action on either of them can produce no effect in that plane. It is, therefore, in consequence of the action of the fluid by which they are surrounded, that the particles have no horizontal motion, and this action must be the same on each, or motion would ensue in the direction of the greater force.

Since fluids press equally in all directions, and the

horizontal pressures on the particles cannot be but equal, the vertical pressures on them, which are, as the distances B D, A C, below the surface of the fluid, must, therefore, be equal.

Therefore, B D = A C; but B D is parallel also to A C, and therefore D C is parallel to B A, and is consequently horizontal.

And since the line joining any two particles in the surface of a fluid is horizontal, the surface itself is horizontal.

If a vessel with vertical sides and horizontal bottom be filled with a fluid, the pressure on the bottom is equal to the weight of the fluid.

Since the sides are vertical, the whole of the fluid may be conceived to be made up of vertical straight lines of fluid particles, each of these lines will press vertically on the base of the vessel, and the sum of these vertical pressures will be the weight of the fluid in the vessel.

The pressure, therefore, on the base = the weight of the fluid.

It might be proved in the same manner that if any plane surface be immersed horizontally in a fluid, the pressure on its upper surface equals the weight of the superincumbent column of fluid.

The pressure of a fluid on any horizontal plane placed in it, is equal to the weight of a column of the fluid whose base is the area of the plane, and whose height is the depth of the plane below the horizontal surface of the fluid.

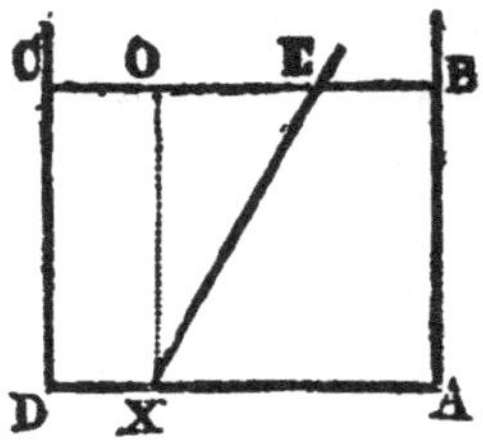

Let A B C D be a vessel with vertical sides and horizontal base, filled with a fluid. The pressure on the base is the weight of the fluid A C.

Let X be any point in the base, and draw X O vertical.

Then the pressures on A X, X D are the weights of the fluids O A and C X.

Now suppose a rigid plate of iron, E X, introduced, this will not affect the pressures on A X and X D, and if A B C D be separated into two vessels, B A X E, E X D C, the pressures are still the same.

Pressure on A X=column B A X O.

Pressure on X D=column O X D C.

That is, so long as the base is horizontal and the vertical height the same, the pressure on equal bases is the same, whether the sides are vertical or not.

For let us consider the separate vessel B A X E. The fluid exerts a positive pressure against X E, for the fluid would spirt out if a hole were made in X E.

X E, then, must exert downwards a pressure equal to this upward pressure of the fluid. Before the iron plate was introduced, this upward pressure supported that part of the fluid X E O.

Therefore, upward pressure on X E=weight of fluid X O E.

Therefore, downward pressure on E X=weight of fluid X O E.

And A X has to sustain not only the weight of the fluid in the vessel, but also the pressure of X E, which is equal to the weight X O E.

That is, it has to sustain a pressure equal to the weight B A X O.

In the vessel E X D C, the portion X O E presses *on E X, and* this is resisted by X E exerting an equal pressure, and neither of these influence the pressure on X D.

Therefore, the only pressure on X D, is the weight O X D C.

Hence, if the bases of three vessels are the same, and their vertical heights equal, and are all filled with the same fluid, the pressures on all their bases are the same.

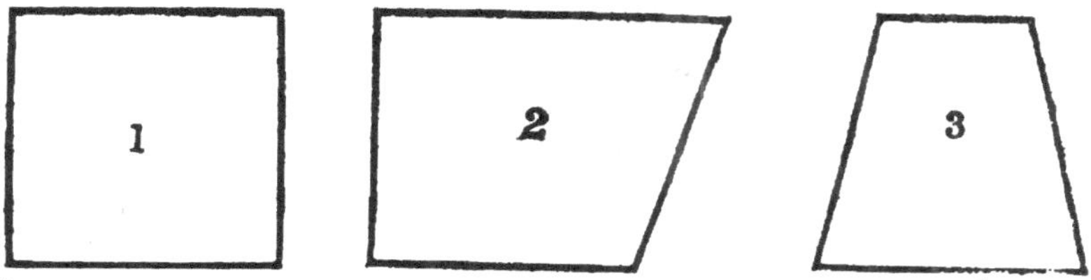

1. Pressure on the base is equal to weight of fluid.
2. Pressure on the base is less than weight of fluid.
3. Pressure on the base is greater than weight of fluid.

To construct and explain the hydrostatic paradox:

a. That any pressure, however small, may, by means of a fluid, be made to balance any other pressure, however great.

b. That any quantity of fluid, however small, by means of its weight, may be made to balance a weight, however large.

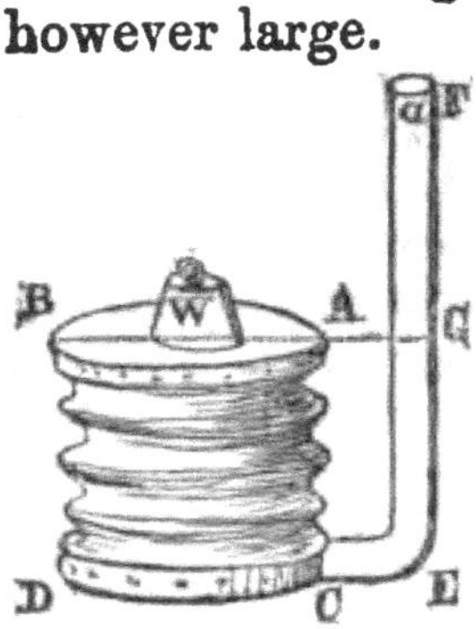

The top and bottom of the vessel, A B C D, consists of two boards, connected by means of leathern sides. The vessel communicates by means of a vertical tube, E F, of a small uniform bore, and a short horizontal pipe, E C.

Let A represent the number of square inches in the area of the board A B, and a the area in square inches of a horizontal section of the pipe E F.

Let water be poured into the tube until it rises to A B. The water will therefore rise in the tube to G, a point in the same horizontal plane with A B.

Now, in a fluid at rest, the pressures on equal areas in the same horizontal plane are equal, and any additional pressure applied to the area (a of the tube) at G will be transmitted undiminished to every equal area throughout the fluid; therefore pressure on area A in B A is equal to the number of areas that (a, the area of the small tube) is contained in A, the area of A B, or pressure on area A of A B : pressure on the area a at G $=$ A : a.

Let w be the weight in pounds of the fluid column F C, and W the weight placed A B.

$$\text{Then, } W : w = A : a$$

$$\therefore w = W \times \frac{a}{A}$$

Thus, any two weights (W, w) may be made to balance each other, by so constructing the apparatus that the areas are in the same proportion as the weights.

It is of no consesequence whether the pressure on the area a at G be produced by a fluid column, or by a piston fitting water-tight, and acted on by some force. The pressures on the areas a at G, and A at A B, will still bear to each other the ratio of a to A; a ratio which is independent of the quantity of fluid contained in the vessel.

BRAMAH HYDROSTATIC PRESS.

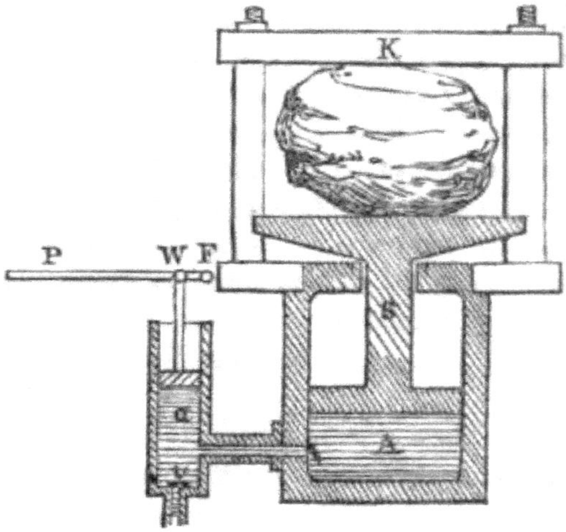

The Bramah press is constructed on this principle. The main points of this machine are as follows: *a* is a small cylinder, and A a large one, communicating one with the other by means of a pipe. Water stands in both cylinders (*a* and A). The piston S fits so as to exclude any water passing to the top; and this is done by a leather fitting round the edge. Between the top of the piston S and the strong framework K, the substance to be compressed is placed. In the smaller cylinder a solid piston is worked by means of a lever, F W P, of which F W is the short arm; in the ascent of the smaller piston, water is admitted into the small cylinder at the valve *v*; in its descent it presses on the surface of the water in *a*, and this pressure is transmitted with equal force throughout the entire mass of the fluid. The piston S is pressed upwards by a force proportioned to the area. If the cylinder, *a*, of the force-pump has an area of $\frac{1}{2}$ an inch, and the area of the large piston 100 inches, then the pressure of the water on the under side of the large piston will be 200 times that in *a*.

And if we suppose the arms of the lever to be as 1 to 30, and at the extremity of the lever at P a force of 50 lbs. is exerted, then the piston in *a* will descend with a pressure of $50 \times 30 = 1500$ lbs., and this multiplied by 200, the area of the large piston will equal 300,000 lbs., the upward pressure of the large piston. In this calculation no allowance has been made by the loss of power by friction.

Let areas of the two pistons be represented by *a* and *b*.

Let *a* be the area of the smaller and *b* the larger.

Let Q be the upward pressure on S, when the smaller piston descends with a force F, then

$$Q : F = b : a$$

For the pressure F is transmitted to every portion of area equal to *a* on the under surface of S; and to every such unit of area a pressure is transmitted equal to $\frac{F}{a}$, and as the lower surface of the large piston contains *b* units, the whole upward pressure on S is $\frac{F b}{a}$, but Q denotes the pressure.

$$\therefore Q = \frac{F b}{a}, \text{ that is, } Q : F - b : a$$

If a body floats in a fluid it displaces as much fluid as is equal to the weight of the body, and it presses downwards, and is pressed upwards with a force equal to the weight of the fluid displaced.

When a body floats, the forces acting are the weight of the body, and the resultant of the pressures upon the surface of the body. But this resultant is evidently vertical, and is the same as when the space occupied by the immersed part of the solid is occupied by fluid. This resultant pressure is ∴ the weight of the fluid displaced.

Hence, as there is equilibrium, the weight of the body = weight of fluid displaced.

When a body floats on a fluid, the line joining the centres of gravity of the body and the fluid are in the same vertical line.

Let G and g be the two centres of gravity. The weight of the fluid displaced acts in a vertical line through g, and as this is supported by the upward pressure of the fluid, this pressure must also act in the vertical line through g.

It may be proved that this upward pressure must act in the vertical line through G, for it supports the weight of the body which acts in that line.

Therefore the vertical lines through G and g are coincident, and G g is a vertical line.

CHAPTER II.

SPECIFIC GRAVITY.

THE specific gravity of a body is the ratio which the weight of any volume of that body bears to the weight of an equal volume of distilled water at a given temperature. If we say that iron has a specific gravity of 7·8, we mean that any volume of iron weighs 7·8 times as much as an equal volume of distilled water. A cubic foot of distilled water weighs 1000 ozs., and from this we can find the weight of any quantity of material whose specific gravity was known.

For instance, suppose we want to find the weight of 3 cubic feet of tin, whose S. G. is 7·3.

A cubic foot of water weighs 1000 ozs.

$\therefore$ A cubic foot of tin weighs $7 \cdot 3 \times 1000$

$\therefore$ 3 cubic feet of tin weighs $7 \cdot 3 \times 3 \times 1000$

And conversely, if the weight of a given volume of a body be known, its specific gravity may be determined.

If M *be the magnitude of a body,* S *its specific gravity, and* W *its weight,* $W = M S$.

If the specific gravity increases in any ratio, the weight of a given bulk or magnitude increases in the same ratio.

Let $M =$ the number of cubic inches in a body, $S =$ specific gravity of the body; that is, let S represent the number of grains that 1 cubic inch of the body weighs.

$W =$ the number of grains the whole body weighs.

$$\text{Then, since } \overset{\text{grns.}}{W} : \overset{\text{grns.}}{S} = \overset{\text{c. in.}}{M} : \overset{\text{c. in.}}{1}$$

$$\therefore W = M \times S$$

The following is a list of the specific gravity of various substances, the standard being pure water:

TABLE OF SPECIFIC GRAVITIES.

Metals.	Weight of Cubic Foot in ounces.	Number of Cubic Inches in a lb.
Antimony, cast	6702	3·8866
Zinc, cast	7190	3·8431
Iron ,,	7207	3·8364
Tin ,,	7291	3·7920
,, hardened	7299	3·7878
Pewter	7471	3·7007
Bar iron	7788	3·5500
Steel, hard	7816	3·5373
,, soft	7833	3·5296
Iron, meteoric / ,, hammered	7965	3·4792
Nickel	8279	3·3395
Brass, cast	8395	3·2933
,, wire	8544	3·2359
Gun metal	8784	3·1476
Copper, cast	8788	3·1461
,, wire	8878	3·1140
,, coin	8915	3·0959
Bismuth, cast	9822	2·8149
Silver, hammered	10510	2·6306
,, coin	10534	2·5733
,, pure	10744	2·6246
Lead, cast	11352	2·4355
Mercury, pure	14000	1·9748
Gold, trinket	15709	1·7600
,, coin	17647	1·6124
,, pure	19258	1·4356
,, hammered	19316	1·4280
Platinum, pure	19500	1·4178
,, hammered	20336	1·3595
,, wire	21041	1·3140

TABLE OF SPECIFIC GRAVITIES—*continued.*

Earth, Stone, &c.	Weight of Cubic Foot in ounces.	Number of Cubic Inches in a lb.
Amber	1078	25·6474
Coal	1250	21·9428
Sand	1500	18·4320
Brick	2000	13·8240
Sulphur	2033	13·5996
Gypsum	2280	12·1263
Porcelain china	2385	11·7351
Stone paving	2416	11·4437
Flint	2594	10·6584
Spar	2594	10·6584
Granite, Aberdeen	2625	10·5325
" Cornish	2662	10·3861
" red	2654	10·4175
Quartz	2640	10·4727
Crystal rock	2653	10·4214
Marble, Egyptian	2668	10·3628
" Parian	2837	9·7455
Slate	2672	10·3473
Chalk	2784	9·9310
Basalt	2864	9·6536
Glass, white	2892	9·5601
" bottle	2733	10·1163
British flint	3329	8·3052
Hornblende	3000	9·2160

Suppose 13 ozs. of lead occupy the same space as 7 ozs. of tin, compare their specific gravities.

Let M be the magnitude of each,

$$\text{Then } 13 \text{ ozs.} = M \times S\,G \text{ lead} \quad \therefore M = \frac{13}{S\,G \text{ of lead}}$$

$$7 \text{ ozs.} = M \times S\,G \text{ tin} \quad \therefore M = \frac{7}{S\,G \text{ of tin}}$$

$$\therefore \frac{13}{S\,G \text{ of lead}} = \frac{7}{S\,G \text{ of tin}}$$

$$\therefore \frac{S\,G \text{ of tin}}{S\,G \text{ of lead}} = \frac{7}{13}$$

What is the weight of two cubic inches of silver?

$$W = M S$$

$$M = 2 \text{ inches, or } \frac{2}{1728} \text{ foot . S G } 10{\cdot}5$$

$$W = \frac{2 \times 1000 \times 10{\cdot}5}{1728} \text{ ounces}$$

What is the weight of a cubical block of stone whose S G is 2·7, and measures 380 feet on one of the sides?

$$W = 380^3 \times 1000 \times 2{\cdot}7 \text{ ounces}$$

If two bodies have the same magnitude M, and if W and W′ be their weights, and S and S′ their specific gravities,

$$W = M S \text{ and } W' = M S'$$

$$\therefore \frac{W}{W'} = \frac{M S}{M S'} = \frac{S}{S'}$$

that is, their specific gravities are directly as their weights.

Also, as an example, we may take two bodies which have the same weight W, and if M and M′ be their magnitudes, and S and S′ their specific gravities,

$$W = M S \text{ and } W = M' S'$$

$$\therefore M S = M' S'.$$

$$\therefore \frac{S}{S'} = \frac{M'}{M}$$

that is, their specific gravities are inversely as their magnitudes.

When a body of uniform density floats on a fluid, the weight of part immersed is to the weight of whole body as the specific gravity of the body is to the specific gravity of the fluid.

Let a solid block of wood of uniform density float on a fluid with M cubic inches above the horizontal surface and N cubic inches below the horizontal surface; and

Let S = the specific gravity of the solid block of wood,

and S′ = the specific gravity of the fluid,

then $(M+N) \times S =$ weight of solid,

$N \times S' =$ the weight of fluid displaced;

but as the body floats these two weights must be equal.

$$\therefore N \times S' = (M+N)\,S : \text{and } \frac{N}{M+N} = \frac{S}{S'},$$

$$\text{or, } N : M+N = S : S'.$$

But $N : M+N$ as the weight of the part immersed is to the weight of the whole body, and ∴ the weight of part immersed is to that of the whole body as the specific gravity of the body is to the specific gravity of the fluid.

When a body is immersed in a fluid, the weight lost in the fluid is to the whole weight of the body as the specific gravity of the fluid is to the specific gravity of the body.

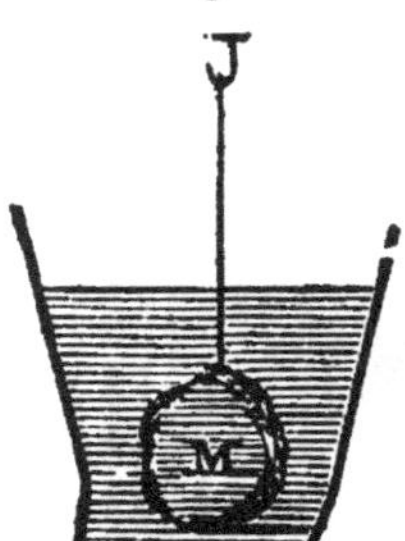

When the body is wholly immersed, the resultant pressure of the fluid vertically upwards is equal to the weight of a volume of fluid equal to that of the body. But this upward pressure diminishes the weight of the body when it is immersed in the fluid, and is the weight lost. Therefore the weight lost in the fluid is equal to the weight of a bulk of the fluid equal to the body, and the specific gravity of the fluid is to the specific gravity of the body as the weight of a bulk of fluid equal to the body is to the weight of the body; that is, as the weight lost is to the whole weight.

Let M S represent the weight of the solid before immersion. Now, after immersion, the weight of the solid is diminished by the resultant upward pressure of the surrounding fluid. This upward pressure is exactly equal to the weight of the displaced fluid, which weight may be represented as M S′. Where S represents the specific gravity of the solid, and S′ the specific gravity of the fluid.

∴ weight lost by the body : the whole weight of body

$$= M\,S' : M\,S = S' : S$$

$$= S\,G \text{ of the fluid} : S\,G \text{ of the body}$$

From this proposition, it appears, that the upward pressure of a fluid on a body wholly immersed is equal to the weight of the displaced fluid.

If this pressure be less than the weight of the body it sinks to the bottom; that is, if the specific gravity of the fluid be less than the specific gravity of the solid.

If the upward pressure of a fluid be greater than the weight of the immersed body—that is to say, if the specific gravity of the fluid be greater than that of the immersed body, the upward pressure will be greater than the downward pressure, and the body will float on the surface of the fluid.

To describe the hydrostatic balance and its use in determining the specific gravity of a body:

1st. When the specific gravity is greater than that of the fluid.

2nd. When the specific gravity is less than that of the fluid.

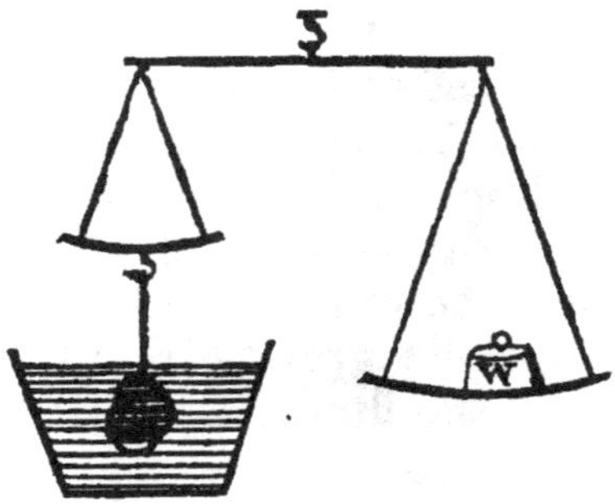

The hydrostatic balance is a common balance with a hook attached to the under part of one of its scale-pans, so that bodies may be weighed either in the usual manner out of the water or in the water.

In order to find the specific gravity of a body heavier than water, and which will therefore sink in water, weigh the body in air and water successively; then the difference of the weights so found is the weight of the water displaced.

Let, as before, the specific gravity of the solid be $= S$
the specific gravity of the fluid $= S'$,

and W, the weight of the body out of the water, as w the weight in the water:

$$\text{Weight lost} - W - w$$

$$\text{Therefore, } W : W - w = S : S'$$

$$\therefore S = \frac{W}{W - w} S'$$

As W and w are known weights, S may be determined when S′ is given.

2. Let the specific gravity be less than that of the fluid.

Let the body be weighed out of the water; then fasten it to a sinker, having previously determined the weight of this sinker in water. Let the sinker and the body be both weighed in water.

It is evident that the weight of the two together in the water will not be so great as the weight of the sinker alone, for the levity of the lighter body will have a tendency to raise itself, and this tendency diminishes the weight in water of the sinker.

Let W be the weight of the body out of the water, Q the weight of the sinker in water, and X the weight of the compound body in water; the levity of the given body is Q − X. Hence Q − X + W is the weight of an equal bulk of fluid, and

$$S = \frac{W}{Q - X + W} S'$$

From this, it appears that the actual weight of the sinker, Q, does not occur, nor is it necessary to know its weight.

The only quantities we have to deal with respecting it, are its weight in the fluid Q, and the levity of the compound body in the water, Q - X.

To describe the common hydrometer, and show how to compare the specific gravity of two fluids by it.

The hydrometer consists of two glass bulbs a, b, attached to each other; from the upper bulb springs a long, uniform, slender stem, which, if produced, would pass through the centres of the two bulbs. The upper bulb is hollow, the lower one is filled with shot or

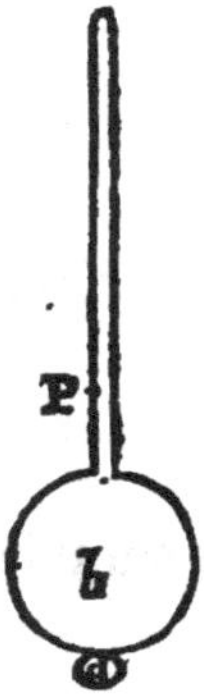

mercury, and serves as a ballast for the instrument, and makes it float steadily in a vertical position. The stem is graduated by divisions of equal lengths.

The hydrometer, bulk for bulk, is lighter than any of the fluids whose specific gravity it is employed to compare, and since the stem is very slender, small variations of the part immersed will occupy a considerable space in the stem, and will be easily ascertained.

Suppose the bulk of the portion of the stem included between two gradations to be one four thousandth part of the bulk of the whole instrument. When the hydrometer is put into a fluid whose specific gravity is S, let 20 divisions be above the surface, and when it is put into another fluid whose specific gravity is S′, let 35 divisions be above the surface.

Now, the weights of the bulks of the two fluids displaced are the same, because each are equal to the weight of the hydrometer.

Let M and M′ be the magnitudes of the displaced fluids.

$$M \times S = \text{weight of hydrometer} = M' \times S'$$

$$\therefore S : S' = M' : M$$

$$= 4000 - 35 : 4000 - 20$$

$$= 3965 : \quad 3980$$

And the ratio of the specific gravities of the two fluids is thus determined.

A mark, P, is made on the stem of the instrument, at the point to which it sinks in proof spirit, which is a mixture of equal weights of pure water and alcohol. Now, alcohol is much lighter than water, and *if a mixture* of these two fluids contain a greater weight of alcohol than of water, it will be lighter than an equal bulk of proof spirit, and the hydrometer will displace a greater bulk of it than it does of proof spirit.

The surface of such a mixture would rise above the point P, as in such a case would be above proof. But if the weight of water be greater than that of the alcohol, the hydrometer will not sink to P, and the mixture is below proof.

Examples.

1. A body weighs 926 grains in air and 320 in water. What is its specific gravity?

2. A body weighed 16 grains in air and 12 in water. What was its specific gravity?

3. What is the weight of a marble statue which contains $1\frac{1}{2}$ cubic feet of marble?

4. What is the weight of 3 cubic feet of Cornish granite?

5. What is the specific gravity of a piece of wood which weighed 14 ozs., and when attached to a sinker caused a loss of 3 ozs.?

6. What is the weight of a piece of paving-stone 2 feet by 3 feet 6, and 3 inches thick?

7. What is the weight of a block of stone 3 feet by 2 feet 6, and 2 feet thick, whose specific gravity is 2·7?

8. A piece of wood, the weight of which was 2984 grains, when attached to a sinker lost in weight 584 grains. What was the specific gravity of the wood?

9. A body weighs 350 grains, and sinks to the same depth when immersed either in water or spirits of wine when loaded with 60 and 15 grains respectively. What is the specific gravity of the spirits of wine?

10. If 20 cubic inches of antimony be mixed with 30 cubic inches of bismuth, what is the specific gravity of the compound?

11. If 30 cubic inches of copper be mixed with 15 inches of zinc, what is the specific gravity of the compound?

12. What is the weight of a copper globe whose radius is 9 inches?

13. A piece of iron weighing 3 lbs. 3 ozs. in the air, and 2 lbs. 9 ozs. in water, is attached to a piece of wood; the two weigh 3 lbs. 12 ozs. in air and 19 ozs. in water. What is the specific gravity of the wood?

14. A body weighs 620 grains in air and 231 in water. What is its specific gravity?

15. If 220 grains of gold be mixed with 2 lbs. 8 ozs. of copper, what is the specific gravity of the compound?

16. What is the weight of a block of copper 9 inches long, 7 inches broad, and $1\frac{1}{2}$ inches thick?

CHAPTER III.

ELASTIC FLUIDS.

The air has weight: this is proved by experiment. The weight of a vessel from which the air has been exhausted is less than when it was filled with air.

The elastic force of the air at a given temperature varies as its density. This may be proved by experiment.

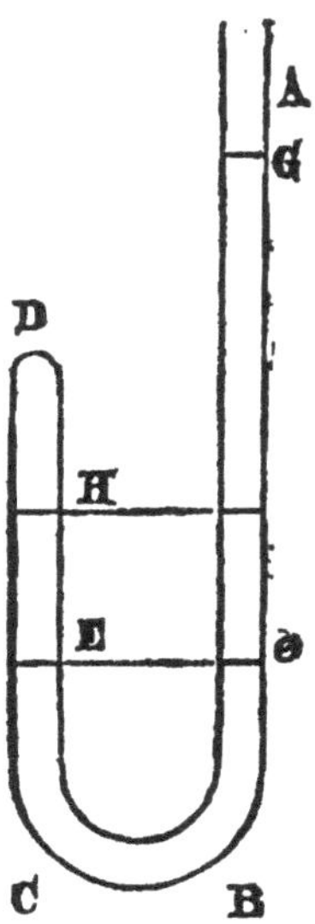

Let A B C D be a graduated tube of uniform bore, having the legs A B, C D parallel.

The end A is open, and D is capable of being opened and closed at pleasure.

Place the tube in a vertical position.

Pour mercury in at the end A, and by opening D make it stand at the same height, E and e, in the limbs D C and A B. Now let D be closed, and again pour in mercury at A, then it will stand at unequal heights G and H in the limbs A B, C D. Let h be the height of the mercury in the barometer at the time of making the experiment. If the volumes D H and D E be determined, which may be done by weighing the mercury they would respectively contain; and if the perpendicular height G H be measured, it is always found that

$$\frac{h + GH}{h} = \frac{\text{vol. } DE}{\text{vol. } DH}$$

Now let P represent the pressure of the air on E when the first quantity of mercury was poured in. This is, of course, the same as the pressure of the atmosphere on the same surface, since D was open at the time. Also let P′ represent the pressure of the air at H, after the second quantity of mercury was poured in. Then if s represent the specific gravity of mercury, the weight of a column h will equal sh (see page 107), but this, as shown below (page 119), is equal to the pressure of the atmosphere on the same surface = P. Again, since there is equilibrium at H, it is evident that P′ (the pressure of the air on H) is equal to the pressure of the atmosphere on G, together with the weight of the column of mercury G H.

And the weights of these are respectively sh, s G H.

$$\therefore \frac{P}{P'} = \frac{sh}{sh + s\,GH}$$

$$= \frac{sh}{s\,(h + GH)}$$

$$= \frac{h}{h + GH}$$

$$= \frac{\text{Vol. DH}}{\text{Vol. DE}} = \frac{\text{density of air in DE}}{\text{density of air in DH}}$$

That is, the pressure of the air varies directly as the density.

This law was discovered by Boyle in 1662, and is named after him, Boyle's law.

The elastic force of air increases by an increase of temperature.

This is easily proved. Let a bladder be partially filled with air, and turned by a roasting-jack, or other means, for a few minutes before the fire; the bladder becomes filled out, and, if the experiment be continued, will burst from the expansion of the included air. But if it be removed into a lower temperature, the included air cools down, occupies less space, and the bladder becomes loose.

To describe the construction of the air-pump and its operation:

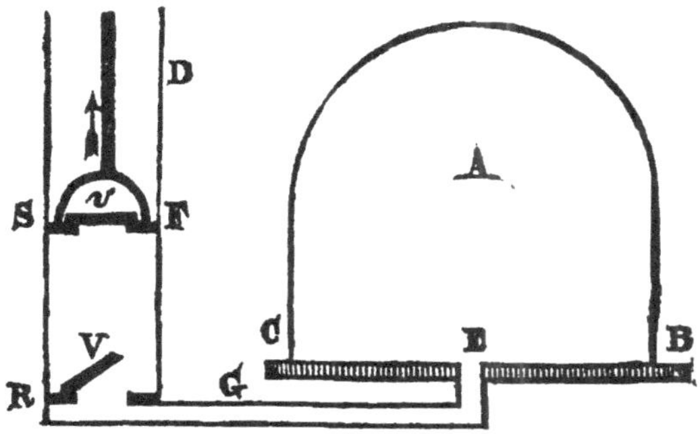

The air-pump consists of a close glass vessel marked A; this glass vessel is called the receiver, and it stands on a metallic plate B C, so accurately as to be air-tight. The tube, G E, connects the receiver with a cylinder, R S, called the barrel. At the bottom of the barrel there is a valve, V, opening upwards, and a piston, F, which also contains a valve opening upwards, and working air-tight in the barrel.

Operation: Suppose the piston F to be at its highest point, and the receiver filled with air of the same density as that of the surrounding atmosphere:

When the piston descends the air in the barrel is

condensed, and as it cannot pass through the lower valve V, which opens upwards, the upper valve *v* opens as soon as this compression exceeds the pressure of the surrounding air which presses on the upper side of the valve *v*. On raising the piston the external air keeps *v* closed, and there being no air in F R, the pressure on the under side of the valve V, communicating with the receiver, opens and allows the air to flow into the barrel. The piston descends again; the air in S R, being condensed, closes the valve V and opens the valve *v*, and so escapes. On the piston ascending, more air flows into the barrel, and this process is repeated until the air in the receiver is so rare as to be unable to open the valve V. The interior of the receiver is, under such circumstances, nearly a vacuum.

To describe the construction of the condenser and its operation:

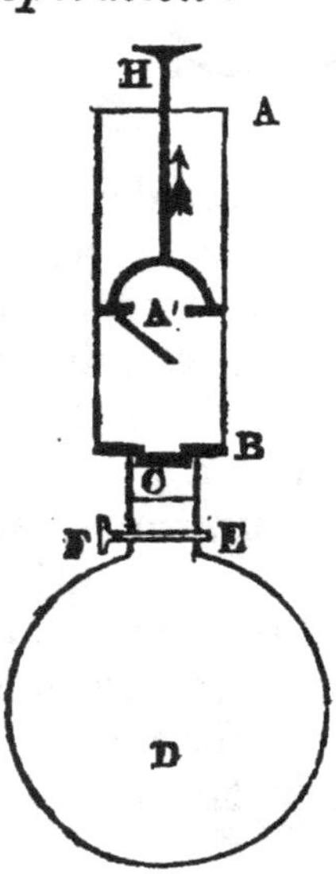

The condenser consists of a barrel and piston, with valves opening the contrary way to those of the air-pump.

Let A B be the barrel, and at C the valve opening inwards, A′ the piston with its valve opening inwards, and B F the pipe communicating with the receiver D. The piston A, being in its highest position, is forced to its lowest position by the handle H. During its descent no air escapes through the valve in A; and the air in A B is driven through the valve at C, and increases the quantity in D. The piston then ascends, and no air escapes from D by the valve at C, because the valve opens inwards, but air enters the barrel A B by the valve at A.

The piston is again forced down, and the air in the barrel A B is driven into the receiver D, as before, and so on.

The pipe B F has a stop-cock E, and when this is closed the pump may be taken off, and the receiver D is filled with condensed air.

To explain the construction of the barometer, and to show that the mercury in the tube is sustained by the pressure of the air on the surface of the mercury in the basin:

The barometer is a glass tube, closed at one end; being filled with a fluid, generally mercury, it is inverted with its open end in a cistern of the same fluid. In any place the fluid stands at a certain height if the tube be long enough.

The upper part of the tube P B is a vacuum.

Let P be the surface of the mercury in the tube A B, and let C D be a portion of the area of the liquid in the cistern equal to the internal area of a horizontal section of the tube A B.

The weight of mercury is equal to the pressure downwards of a column of mercury C P, arising from its weight. The pressure downwards on the area A C is equal to the pressure upwards on A C, which equals the pressure upwards on C D, since A C and C D are equal areas in the same horizontal plane. The fluid being at rest, the pressure of the air downwards on C D is equal to the weight of the column of mercury C P, supported in the tube of the barometer by the downward pressure of the atmosphere on the surface of the mercury.

It has been shown that the pressure of a fluid on a horizontal plane immersed in it was equal to the weight of a column of the fluid whose base is equal to the area of the plane, and whose height is the depth of the plane below the surface of the fluid. The pressure then exerted by the atmosphere on such an area is measured by the weight of a vertical column of mercury of equal area to the barometer-tube, and whose weight is the vertical height of the mercury in the tube.

As the pressure of the air is measured by the weight of a column of the fluid which it supports, the barometer-tube might be filled with water, oil, spirits of wine, or any fluid whatever, but as mercury is the heaviest known fluid, it is generally used, because the column which measures a given pressure is much shorter than if any other fluid were employed. It takes about 30 inches of mercury to balance the pressure of the atmosphere, and since mercury is 13·6 times heavier than water, it would take a column of water to make a water-barometer $13{\cdot}6 \times 30$ inches = or a column of water 34 feet high, to produce the same effect.

To find the pressure of the atmosphere on a horizontal square inch of surface, when the column of mercury stands at 30 inches and the area of the tube equals one square inch.

The weight of a cubic foot of water is 1000 ozs. $\therefore$ weight of a cubic foot of mercury is $1000 \times 13{\cdot}6$ ozs.

1 cubic foot or $12 \times 12 \times 12$ cubic inches : 30 inches $= 1000$ ozs. $\times 13{\cdot}6$: to weight in ounces of 30 inches *of mercury*, which $= \dfrac{13600 \times 13{\cdot}6}{12 \times 12 \times 12} = 236$ozs. of $14\frac{3}{4}$lbs.

The pressure of the atmosphere will, therefore, be greater or less, according to the height at which the column of mercury stands in the barometer tube. It appears, then, by this reasoning, that every square inch of horizontal surface is pressed by the atmosphere with a force of near 15 lbs. A piece of note paper 7 inches by 5 will sustain a pressure of $7 \times 5 = 35 \times 15 =$ 455 lbs. The reason why the paper is not torn to pieces by this pressure, is explained by the fact that the pressure is counterbalanced by an equal upward pressure on the under side.

The air being an elastic fluid is much more dense on the surface of the earth than at the top of a high mountain, because the stratum of the atmosphere resting on the surface of the earth has to sustain the weight of the mass above it.

The atmosphere is supposed to extend about 45 miles. We have seen that a vertical column of water 34 or 35 feet high, and a column of mercury 29 or 30 inches high, and a column of the atmosphere as high as it reaches—45 miles—all weigh the same, provided the horizontal sections of these columns are of the same area. Now the heights of these columns of water and mercury will vary, according to the varying pressure of the atmosphere. In a dense atmosphere, which generally looks bright and clear, the mercury ascends; in a light atmosphere, when the mists, smoke, and vapour fall through the atmosphere to the surface of the earth, the mercury falls. From these indications people predict the kind of weather we are likely to have; hence barometers are frequently called weather-glasses, but what they really do show is the varying pressure of the atmosphere.

To explain the action of the siphon:

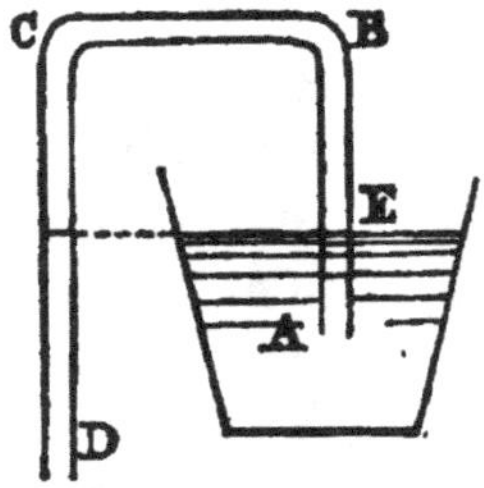

The siphon is a bent tube, open at both ends, with limbs of unequal length.

Suppose A B C D to be a tube of uniform bore, and the two limbs A B and C D parallel and connected at right angles by the tube B C.

If the tube A B C D be filled, by pouring in water at the end D till it runs out at A, then stopping that end with the thumb, fill the other limb to the top, stop that end and invert it in a vessel of water or other liquid, placing it so that the vertical height of D C is greater than that of E B, E being the point where the tube meets the surface of the liquid. Let the end A and D be now opened by the removal of the thumb and finger employed to close the ends.

Upward pressure within the tube at E = the atmospheric pressure, and the downward pressure at E = the column of fluid E B.

Therefore, the whole remaining pressure at E tending to push the fluid in the E B C D, is equal to the atmospheric pressure, minus the weight of the column of water E B.

And similarly the upward pressure at D, tending to force the fluid in the direction D C B A, is equal to the atmospheric pressure, minus the pressure of the column of water D C.

But the pressure of the column D C is greater than that of E B, because the vertical height of D C is greater than that of E B. The upward pressure at E is only opposed by the column E B, and will be greater than that at D, which is opposed by the longer column D C, and will therefore overcome that at D, and the fluid will move in the direction A B C D.

If the fluid used be water, it is necessary that the

vertical height E B be less than 34 feet, otherwise the atmosphere could not support the column E B, and the siphon would not operate. In such a case the downward pressure at E would be greater than the upward pressure, so that there would be no pressure to move the fluid through the siphon.

It is not necessary, although more convenient, that the limb D C should be longer than B A. All that is necessary is that the vertical height of D C should be greater than the vertical height of E D.

To show how to graduate a common thermometer :

No. 57

The freezing point of water and the boiling point of water are fixed in position.

The common thermometer is an instrument consisting of a bulb, and a slender stem of uniform bore, containing a fluid (mercury or spirits of wine); the former for high temperatures, and the latter generally for low temperatures. These fluids expand by heat and contract by cold, so that its surface is always in the tube. The part above the surface of the mercurial column is a vacuum.

Let the thermometer be first placed in melting snow; the point at which the mercury becomes stationary is marked as the freezing point. Next let the thermometer be placed in vapour of water boiling under a given atmospheric pressure; the point at which the mercury ceases to rise is marked as the boiling point.

For Fahrenheit's division, divide the space between the freezing and boiling points into 180 equal parts, and continue the scale of equal parts upwards and downwards. Place 32 at the freezing point and 0 at 32 parts below the freezing point, and 212 at the boiling point.

For a centigrade thermometer, divide the space between the freezing and boiling points into 100 equal parts, marking the freezing point 0 and the boiling point 100.

To reduce the degrees of a thermometer in Fahrenheit's scale to a centigrade and the converse.

To reduce a Fahrenheit to a centigrade, subtract 32, which gives the number of degrees above the freezing point, and multiply by $\frac{5}{9}$, because 180° Fahrenheit are equal to 100 centigrade.

Thus, 59° F. = 27 F. above freezing, or 32° F. =

$$\frac{5 \times 27^\circ}{9} = 15 \text{ centigrade.}$$

To reduce centigrade to Fahrenheit, multiply by $\frac{9}{5}$, which gives the number of degrees Fahrenheit above the freezing point, and add 32, which gives the number above Fahrenheit's zero.

Thus, 60 centigrade = 90 F. above freezing point = 90 F. + 32 F. = 122 F.

To explain the construction of the siphon-gauge :

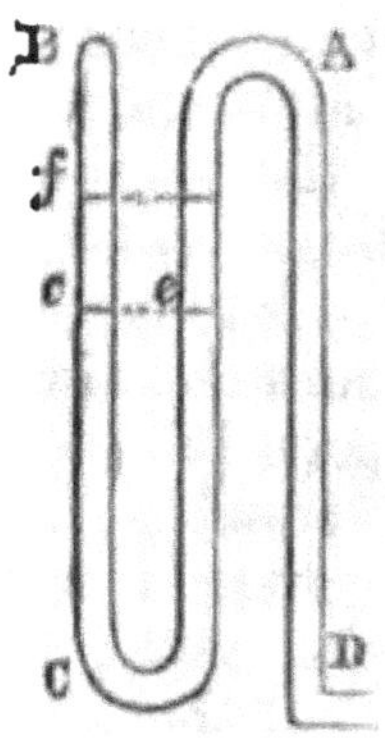

The siphon-gauge is a bent glass tube, closed at B, and containing a fluid, generally mercury, and fixed to an air-pump or other machine to determine the rarefaction of the air.

Let A B C D be the siphon-gauge fixed to a pipe communicating with the receiver of an air-pump ; let *e* C *c* *f* be a portion of the tube filled with mercury, B *f* being a vacuum ; then the vertical height of *f* above *e* measures the density of the air in D A *e*. If D A *e* were a vacuum, that is, if the exhaustion of the air-pump were perfect, *e* and *f* would be in the same horizontal line.

To describe the construction of a common pump and its operation:

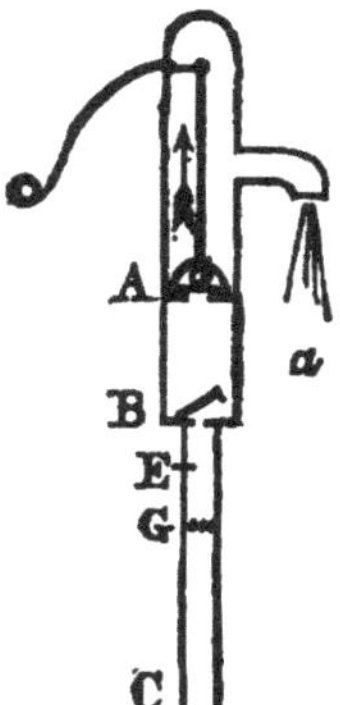

The common pump consists of a cylindrical barrel, A B, closed at the bottom, B, by means of a valve opening upwards. From B, a pipe passes downwards to the well at C, and the water which rises above the piston is delivered by the spout. The operation of the pump is very simple. The piston, A, being in its lowest position, is raised to its highest position by means of the handle, which is a lever. As the valve at *d* opens upwards, no air is admitted at *d* during its ascent, and as the valve at B opens upwards, the air which occupied the pipe and barrel follows the piston in its ascent, and its pressure on the surface of the water at the bottom of the pipe is diminished, and the water rises in the pipe by the pressure of the atmosphere on the surface of the well. Suppose by the first ascent of the piston the water rises to G, the piston then descends to its lowest position, the valve at B is closed, therefore the air in G B remains the same, and the water remains at G, while the air in B A escapes by the valve at *d*.

The piston is again raised, the air expands in G B as before, and the surface of the water at G now rises to E. The same operation being repeated, the water will again rise till it passes into the barrel of the pump through the valve at B. The piston now descends and presses on the water in the barrel, and as the water cannot escape it opens by its pressure the valve at *d*, and in the ascent of the piston the water is lifted and the valve at *d* closes, while the valve at B opens and the water on the upper side of the piston is delivered out at the spout of the pump. In describing the common pump, remember that—

When the piston ascends, the lower valve opens and the upper valve closes. When the piston descends, the lower valve closes and the upper valve opens.

To describe the construction and operation of a force pump:

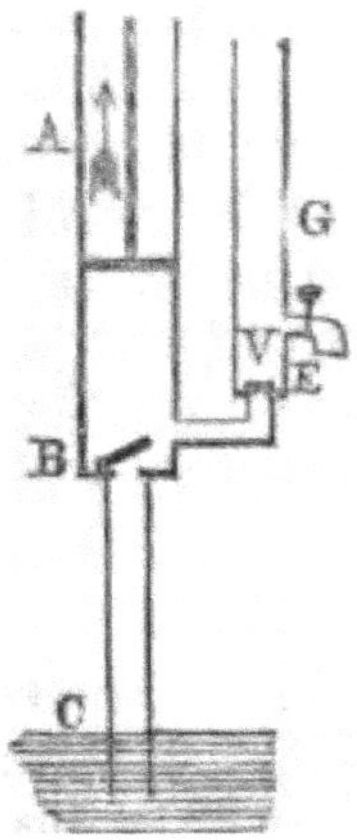

The forcing-pump consists of a cylindrical barrel, A B, closed at the bottom, B, by means of a valve which opens upwards, and a piston with no valve, and a spout, E, above the upward opening valve, V. By turning the tap the water cannot escape at E, and, therefore, ascends the pipe G F. The pipe B C descends to the well.

The operation of the pump is as follows:

The piston, in ascending from its lowest to its highest position, draws the water after it, as in a common pump. When the piston descends, the air is expelled at the valve V, and escapes at the spout. After a few strokes of the piston the water ascends into the barrel through the valve at B. When the piston descends it presses on the surface of the water in the barrel, and forces it through the valve V, and continues at every succeeding stroke upwards to draw the water through the valve at B, and force it through the valve V in its descent.

To describe the operation of a fire-engine:

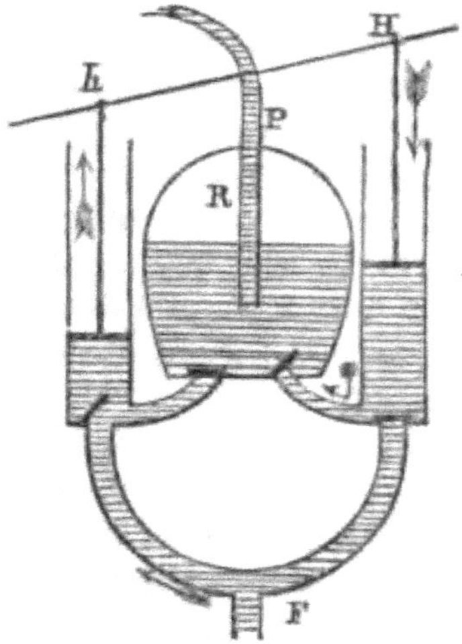

The fire-engine consists of two force-pumps, each of which communicates with the suction-hose, F, which passes either into a well or pond, or is attached, as in large towns, to the main water pipes.

Each of the pumps forces water into the receiver, R, into which a pipe, P, passes nearly to the bottom; to the upper part of the pipe is screwed a flexible hose, and at the end of this hose is the jet.

By the action of the pumps the water enters the receiver, and when it reaches above the under part of the pipe, the air in the receiver, not being able to escape, becomes condensed by the admission of every fresh quantity of water into the receiver, which by its elasticity forces the water up the hose, and is thrown out with great force at the jet. Before this action has ceased a fresh quantity of water is forced into the receiver, the air is again condensed by this means, the stream is rendered continuous instead of being thrown out in distinct jets.

If the air in the receiver is so condensed that its elastic force can just support a column of water whose height is equal to the vertical height of the jet above the level of the water in the receiver, together with the atmospheric pressure at the top of the jet, the water will just rise to the top, but will not, as is obvious, be thrown out unless the air in the receiver is more condensed, or, what amounts to the same thing, the column shortened.

It is this extreme condensation necessary to throw the water that makes the working of the engine very difficult; the pistons are worked by the lever H *h*, so that when one ascends the other descends; the figure represents the ascent of *h* and the descent of H, and the open valves show the direction in which the water is flowing.

To describe the operation of the lifting pump:

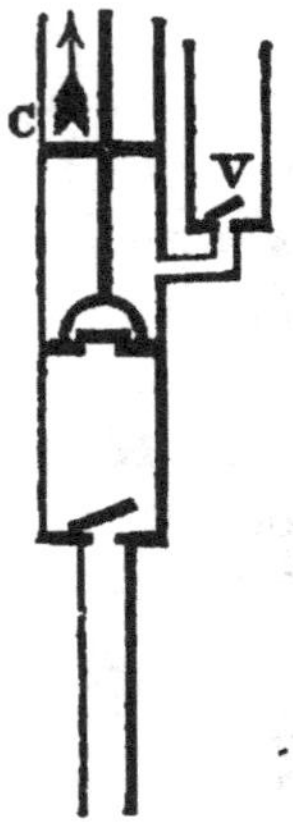

This consists of a common pump, with a valve at V.

The piston-rod works in an air-tight collar at C; by a moment's inspection it will be easily understood the figure represents the ascent of the piston.

THE HYDRAULIC RAM.

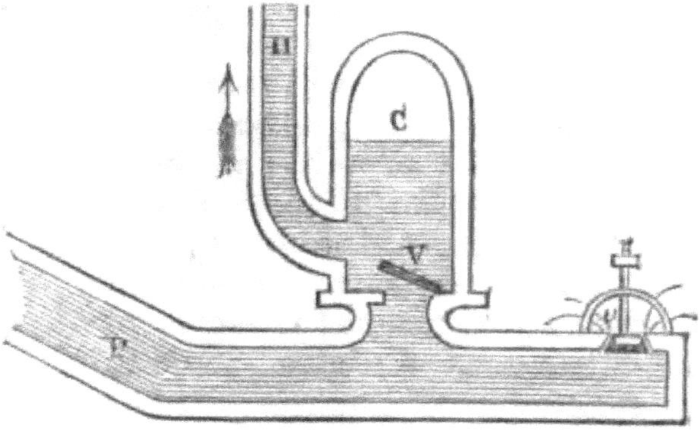

When a flow of water in a pipe is suddenly stopped, a considerable force is generated by the momentum of the water. The operation of this principle is familiar to those who obtain water for domestic purposes by means of pipes from an elevated cistern or reservoir. The sudden stoppage of the flow by turning the cock quickly is attended with a jarring in the pipes. This is due from the sudden change from a state of motion to a state of rest. This property has been usefully applied in the construction of the hydraulic ram. A valve, *v*, opening downwards allows the water to escape, and so produces a current down the pipe P; the fluid acquires in its flow a sufficient force to close *v*; the motion is thus suddenly stopped. This causes a reaction, which produces a pressure sufficient to open the valve V, and a portion of water enters into the chamber C. The current having spent its force, the valve v falls by its own weight, by which means the current again flows towards v. The pressure at V being removed, that valve falls and closes the opening into C. The machine is now in the same condition as at first. The water again acquires a momentum, which closes v and forces more of it into C, and so the action is continued so long as the supply of water is maintained.

A very small descent will raise a column of water a considerable height in H. The flow should be regular, as the weight of the valve v is adjusted to the quantity of water, and the pipe P should be a good length, or a portion of the water is thrown back every time into the reservoir. The space C is an air chamber, which performs the same office as in the fire-engine, viz. keeps up a steady supply from the pipe H, or its action would be spasmodic.

THE ARCHIMEDIAN SCREW.

This screw is said to have been invented by Archimedes for the purpose of draining land in Egypt; others ascribe the invention to the Egyptians. It consists of a hollow spiral tube wound round an axis and turned by means of a handle. As the end of the tube dips into the water it is filled with the fluid, which rises up the tube at every successive revolution. As the screw during its motion changes from a lower to a higher position, the water falls backwards, but is at the same time lifted to a higher position, so that it gradually ascends and is discharged at the upper end.

THE CHAIN PUMP.

The chain pump is said to have been invented by *the Chinese.* As it is not so likely to be choked with sand as ordinary pumps with leather valves, it is chiefly used in ships. The pump consists of a square box and two wheels, and a number of square boards or buckets joined together by a chain. The buckets fit the box so as to move with very little friction. The lower wheel merely guides the buckets, but the upper wheel revolves. Each bucket as it enters the box lifts up the water above it and discharges it at the top.

MERCURIAL STEAM GAUGE.

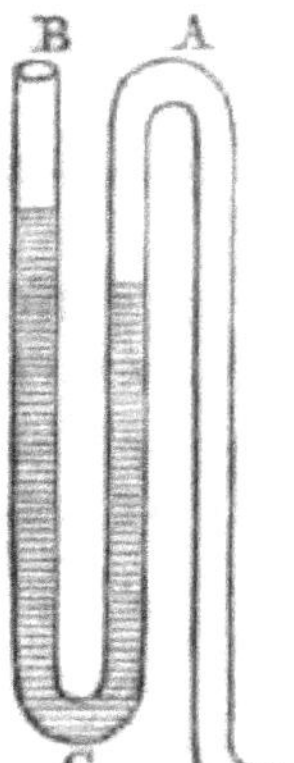

This arrangement is frequently used in low-pressure steam-engines to show the elastic force of the steam in the boiler. One end of the D tube has a free communication with the steam in the boiler, and the other end is open to the atmosphere. The pressure of the steam forees the mercury down the limb A C and up the limb C B. Let us suppose the mercury in both limbs to be in the same horizontal line, then the pressure of the steam is just equal to the atmospheric pressure. If the level of the mercury in A B C is above the level of the mercury in A C, then the pressure of steam exceeds that of the atmosphere; and this difference of pressure may be determined by observing the difference of the level of the mercurial column in both limbs, allowing a pressure of one pound on every square inch for every two inches in the difference of level. If the column of mercury in the tube B C falls below the level of the mercury in the tube A C, the atmospheric pressure exceeds that of the steam, and the excess may be determined in the same way.

Examination of Science Schools and Classes, *17th May,* 1861.

THEORETICAL MECHANICS.

General Instructions.

Three hours are allowed for this paper.

You are only permitted to attempt twelve questions.

You may select your questions from Series I., or from Series II., or from both.

The value attached to the correct answer of each question is marked against it.

N.B.—A full and exact answer will in all cases gain more marks than an inexact or incomplete answer; though in the former case the question may be the more easy of the two and have less marks attached to it.

Series I.

1. Explain the meaning of the terms *Gravity, Weight, Tension.* (10.)
2. A weight of 10 lbs. is supported on a horizontal rod, which weighs 2 lbs. and is suspended by 2 vertical strings fastened to its extremities. The rod is 12 ft. long, and the weight is 2 ft. 6 in. from one end. What are the tensions of the strings? (10.)
3. How would you explain the meaning of *centre of gravity* of a body? Show how to find the centre of gravity of a board in the shape of a *triangle.* (10.)

4. Define *velocity*, *accelerating force*, *momentum*. How is accelerating force measured? (10.)
5. Write down the third law of motion; and give reasons for assuming it to be true. (10.)
6. What is the fundamental law of fluid pressure? How would you show it to be true? Describe an experiment. (10.)
7. Show that the surface of a fluid at rest must be horizontal. (10.)
8. What are the conditions of equilibrium of a floating body? Show that they are necessary and sufficient. (16.)
9. What is the difference between *elastic* and *non-elastic* fluids? Describe an experiment to show that in elastic fluids the pressure is proportional to the density. (16.)
10. How is the pressure of the atmosphere determined? Describe a common barometer. (16.)
11. What is the principle of *virtual velocities?* Show, in a lever, that what is gained in power is lost in time. (16.)
12. A weight of 3 tons has to be raised by means of a screw. The distance between its threads is half an inch. It is worked by a lever whose length is 3 ft. from the central axis of the screw. What power must be applied (friction to be neglected)? (12.)

Series II.

13. If three forces acting on a point keep it at rest, show that they are represented in relative magnitude, and in direction, by the sides of a triangle, drawn under certain conditions. State

what those conditions are, and prove the proposition. (20.)

14. Define a *moment*, or a *couple*. When several forces act upon a body and keep it at rest, what mechanical conditions exist among them? (20.)

15. Show that a body falling freely under the action of gravity from rest will in the fifth second describe a space nine times as great as the space it described in the first second. (16.)

16. A weight of 4 lbs. hangs vertically by a string which passes over a pulley and is attached to another weight of 6 lbs. resting on an inclined plane whose rise is 1 in 3: the string remains parallel to the plane during the motion. Find the accelerating force and the tension of the string. (16.)

17. Explain what is meant by centrifugal force, and show how it is measured. (20.)

18. When a vessel is filled with fluid, what is the measure of the pressure on its horizontal base? Give reasons for your answer. (12.)

19. What is the relation between pressure and velocity when a fluid is in motion in a full closed tube? Explain your answer by numerical illustrations. (16.)

20. How is the barometer used for calculating heights above the sea level? (16.)

21. Why do rollers help in the moving of great weights? Explain their mechanical action. Give instances of friction as a useful resistance. (20.)

22. When a pendulum is set vibrating, why does it not stop when it comes to the lowest point? A chandelier hangs from a high roof, and is

itself 20 ft. from the ground: it makes 5 vibrations in 41 seconds. What is the height of the roof? (20.)

23. Find the weight of a stone which when placed upon a block of wood (weighing 523 ounces) will just cause it to sink in water. Specific gravity of wood = ·596. (30.)

24. What is the form of the curve in which a flexible body hangs between two points? Why can it never be straight? (20.)

Examination of Science Schools and Classes,
18th May, 1861.

APPLIED MECHANICS.

General Instructions.

Three hours are allowed for this paper.

You are only permitted to attempt twelve questions.

You may select your questions from Series I., or from Series II., or from both.

The value attached to the correct answer of each question is marked against it.

N.B.—A full and exact answer will in all cases gain more marks than an inexact or incomplete answer; though in the former case the question may be the more easy of the two and have less marks attached to it.

Series I.

1. Describe and explain the construction of a common steelyard. (10.)
2. When a nail is being drawn with a pair of pincers show how the forces act at each point where they are applied. (10.)
3. Describe a good holding mortise-joint. (10.)
4. What is the best form for nails and screws? Give reasons for your answer. (10.)
5. What is the use of the fly-wheel? (10.)
6. Give some simple example of communication of *motion* by wrapping connectors. When flat

belts are used, what is the proper form of the pulley on the shafting? Why? (16.)

7. How do you find the pressure on a lock gate? Is the centre of pressure above or below the centre of gravity of the surface pressed? (16.)
8. Describe contrivances for regulating the admission of steam to the cylinder so as to equalise the velocity. (16.)
9. Explain the action of a common pump. (16.)
10. What is the cause of the tides? Why are they higher in the mouths of rivers, and in arms of the sea, than in the open sea? (10.)
11. Explain the construction and action of door-hinges which make the doors self-closing. (16.)
12. How do the two elastic springs in a common watch act respectively? (16.)

Series II.

13. Explain the mechanism of a good door-lock. (16.)
14. What properties of elastic fluids make them suitable for measures of force? Describe a steam indicator; how can it be made self-recording? (16.)
15. Describe a crane for lifting great weights as it would be constructed on an open quay. (16.)
16. Show how the force of the wind is applied to grind corn. (16.)
17. In the bridge for a travelling crane, show how the tension rods act to increase the strength of the structure. (20.)
18. What is the construction of the hydrometer? How can it be used to detect adulteration of liquids? (20.)

19. What shapes of teeth of wheels will secure regular action between a driver and a follower? Explain how they are found out. (20.)
20. What is meant by the "parallel motion" in a stationary beam engine? What is its object? Does it *entirely* serve that object? (20.)
21. Why does moistening a rope cause it to contract in length? (20.)
22. Describe all the parts of a spanner or screw wrench. (20.)
23. Explain the construction of carriage springs of different forms. (20.)
24. What is a *turbine?* What is the common principle in this machine and the hydraulic ram? (20.)

MECHANICAL PHYSICS.

PAPERS *given to Candidates in the Examination for Science Certificates, held at South Kensington, November*, 1861.

THEORETICAL MECHANICS.—1ST PAPER.

SECTION I.

1. If two forces acting on a point are represented by two straight lines in magnitude and direction, and the parallelogram be completed of which these lines are the adjacent sides, show that the diagonal represents the *magnitude* of the resultant force (assuming that it represents the *direction*).
2. When several forces given in magnitude and direction act simultaneously upon a point, show how we may most conveniently find out the magnitude and direction of a single force which shall counteract their united effect.
3. Explain the equilibrium of a kite balanced in the air. The forces must be represented by lines drawn in the proper directions through the proper points.

SECTION II.

1. Find the centre of parallel forces acting on a body, and explain the result when two forces are equal, parallel, and act in opposite directions.
2. Explain the forces acting on a drawer when you are attempting to pull it out by one handle, and it sticks fast.

3. A round table stands on three equidistant legs, and is loaded with a given weight at a given point. How do you find the pressure exerted on the floor by each leg?

Section III.

1. When pulling out a nail with a pair of pincers, explain all the forces which are called into action.
2. Define the *centre of gravity*, and find that of two spheres touching each other, whose radii are 8 inches and 3 inches respectively, and their densities in the ratio of 5 : 1, the smaller one being the more dense.
3. A cone with its vertex downwards is partly filled with mercury; the depth of the liquid is 6 inches, and the radius of its surface 4 inches. If the temperature is raised 100° Fahrenheit find the rise in the centre of gravity (neglecting the expansion of the vessel, and taking the expansion of the mercury in bulk as ·00010415 for each 1° Fahrenheit).

Section IV.

1. A rectangular mass of iron rests on an inclined plane; it is on the point of sliding down and also of overturning; its base is 2 feet square, and its height 3·08 feet. What is the coefficient of friction?
2. How do we estimate the force exerted by a buttress to support a wall?
3. Enunciate the principle of virtual velocities, and prove it in the case of the lever.

SECTION V.

1. Define momentum, moving force, and velocity. Enunciate the third law of motion.
2. In uniformly accelerated motion, show that the space described from rest varies as the square of the velocity, the force being constant.
3. A body is thrown vertically upwards with a velocity of 150 feet per second: how many seconds will elapse before it is 100 feet from the ground? Explain the double answer.

SECTION VI.

1. A body A, moving at the rate of 10 feet per second meets a body B moving at the rate of 6 feet per second—the mass of A is three times that of B. What is the velocity after impact when the bodies are inelastic?
2. In the previous case, if the coefficient of elasticity is $\frac{1}{3}$, calculate the motion after impact.
3. A weight of 8 lbs. drags one of 2 lbs. by a string passing over a fixed pulley: the strings being parallel, find the velocity of the centre of gravity.

SECTION VII.

1. A pendulum vibrating seconds at the earth's surface is taken down a mine whose depth is one mile: how many vibrations will it make there in 24 hours?
2. A weight of 10 lbs. is suspended by a string of 8 feet: when it is whirled round so as to make three complete revolutions in a second, what is the greatest tension which the string has to bear?

3. What is meant by the permanence of the plane of vibration of a pendulum? What remarkable experiment can be performed to show this?

Section VIII.

1. What is the *centre of percussion?* Show how to find its position in a heavy rod moving about one of its ends.
2. How can a body be made to vibrate in a cycloid?
3. Show how the compound pendulum can be used to find the force of gravity.

THEORETICAL MECHANICS.—2ND PAPER.

SECTION I.

1. What is *vis viva?* Show that the amount of work accumulated in a body moving with a given velocity is one half the *vis viva.*
2. How are the vibrations of thin plates exhibited to the eye? Describe the node lines in some of the simplest instances.
3. What is the form of the curve in which a flexible body will be at rest between two fixed points? Describe it, and mention its principal properties. At what point is the tension greatest?

SECTION II.

1. Show by mathematical reasoning that the pressures at all points in the same horizontal plane within a fluid at rest must be equal. (The only forces acting being gravity and the pressure of the atmosphere.)
2. Describe an apparatus by which the compressibility of water may be measured.
3. Show that the pressure of a fluid on any surface is proportional to the area of the surface and the depth of the centre of gravity of the surface.

SECTION III.

1. A ship is floating in fresh water, A is the area of its plane of flotation, it moves into salt water and the vertical distance between the new and old positions of its plane of flotation is (n) inches. Hence find the weight of the ship,

having given the specific gravities of fresh and salt water.

2. A sphere, radius 3 inches, weighs 50 lbs. in vacuo: what force will support it when immersed in water?
3. What is the *metacentre* of a floating body? Show how it is found, and explain its use in determining the stability.

Section IV.

1. When water escapes from a small orifice, show that the velocity is as the square root of the depth of the orifice below the surface of the fluid.
2. Describe an experiment to show the effect of friction of particles of water in motion, and the lateral exhaustion produced by apertures in pipes filled with moving water.
3. In an open channel where the water flows uniformly at the surface, according to what law does the velocity vary below the surface?

Section V.

1. A piece of wood in vacuo weighs 2 lbs.; when connected with a piece of metal (whose weight in vacuo is 3 lbs., and in water $2\frac{3}{4}$ lbs.) the weight of the compound mass in water is $1\frac{1}{2}$ lbs. Find the specific gravity of the wood and of the metal.
2. Three globes of the same diameter, and of given specific gravities, are placed in the same straight line. How must they be arranged so that they may balance on the same point of the line in *vacuo,* and in water?

3. A semicircular tube with its two extremities in the same horizontal line is filled with equal quantities of fluid of different specific gravities. What quantity of the lighter fluid will be expelled before the equilibrium is established?

Section VI.

1. Define mathematically an *elastic* fluid, and explain the connexion between pressure, temperature, and density.
2. How would you measure the pressure of the atmosphere?
3. If a small quantity of air should get into the vacuum of the barometer tube, how would you calculate its effects on the indications of the barometer (its volume being given at the temperature 0° C.)?

Section VII.

1. Define *specific heat.* How is it measured?
2. Explain clearly why a fall in the barometer should indicate rain, and a rise indicate fair weather.
3. What corrections for temperature are required when you are comparing the indications of a barometer at the base and at the summit of a mountain?

Subdivision II.—Applied Mechanics.

APPLIED MECHANICS.—1st Paper.

Section I.

1. Describe and draw the crown wheel escapement, and explain its action.
2. Describe and draw a reversing motion for a planing machine.
3. By what mechanical contrivance can we secure a slow forward motion of the cutter in a shaping machine, with a rapid motion when the cut is accomplished?

Section II.

1. Give a convenient method for reversing the position of the cutter in a planing machine.
2. In wheel-work, if the teeth of the driver have to act upon round projecting pins in the follower, what is the best shape for the teeth?
3. Describe a good parallel motion. Explain the principle of the *Pantograph*, and show how it is applied in parallel motions.

Section III.

1. Describe Watt's *Steam Indicator*, and explain clearly how the curve described by the pointer is made use of to measure the work done by the engine.
2. What are the objections to Watt's *Governor?* Show how they are obviated in extreme cases

by Slemen's contrivance adapting an epicycle train to a conical pendulum.

Describe the *Snail* wheel used in the striking machinery of clocks, and show how it acts in repeaters.

SECTION IV.

Describe the *Geneva* stop, and show how it is used to prevent overwinding in a watch.

Explain the principle of *Saxton's differential pulleys.*

Describe Hook's joint, and find the relative angular velocities of the pieces.

SECTION V.

Explain the different ways in which materials yield to crushing pressure. What is meant by *ultimate* and *proof strength*, and *working stress?*

What are the results of experiments on the strength of cast-iron columns, solid and hollow?

Define *unit of work, modulus of a machine.* What must be the horse-power of a stationary engine that draws a weight of 150 tons along a level road at the rate of 30 miles an hour?

SECTION VI.

The mean section of a stream is 7 feet by 2 feet; its mean velocity is 30 feet per minute; it has a fall of 20 feet; it is required to raise water to a height of 250 feet by means of a water-wheel whose modulus is ·7. How many cubic feet will it raise per minute?

A train weighing 90 tons comes to the foot of an incline of 1 in 160, with a velocity of 30 miles an hour, the resistances are 7 lbs. per ton, the length of the incline 2 miles, the train has at the top of the incline a velocity of 20 miles per hour. How many units of work have been expended in getting the train up the incline, and through how great a distance would an expenditure of the same number of units have taken the train with a uniform velocity along a horizontal line?

3. When the powder in the bore of a cannon is exploded, the pressure on the end of the bore and on the shot are at each instant equal; a shot weighing 6 lbs. is fired from a gun free to move, and weighing 6 cwt.; the velocity with which the shot leaves the gun is 1000 feet per second. What is the initial velocity of the gun's recoil?

Section VII.

1. A roof has a pitch of 45°, the rafters are 40 feet long, the weight of each square foot of roofing is 18 lbs. Determine the diameter of the wrought-iron tie necessary to hold the feet of the principal rafters with safety, supposing them 10 feet apart (take the tenacity of wrought-iron bar at 67,200 lbs. per square inch).

2. A mass of earth, the specific gravity of which is 1·7, whose surface is horizontal, presses against a revetment wall whose top is on the level of the ground, and height 20 feet, the natural slope of the earth being 45°. Show that the pressure of the earth on each foot of the length of the wall is 3646 lbs.

3. A cylindrical log of wood being given, show that the strongest rectangular beam that can be cut out of it is one whose sides are in the proportion of $1 : \sqrt{2}$.

APPLIED MECHANICS.—2ND PAPER.

SECTION I.

1. Find the whole pressure on a conical vessel filled with fluid with its base downwards.
2. Describe Hare's hydrometer, and show how to compare the specific gravities of two fluids by means of it.
3. Describe and explain the action of Appold's centrifugal pump.

SECTION II.

1. Show how the principle of the siphon is applied to explain the action of intermittent springs.
2. Show how the attraction of the sun and moon on the ocean causes the tides, and explain why there is a tide every twelve hours.

SECTION III.

Describe and explain the action of one of these machines:

1. The moderator lamp.
2. A spring roller blind.
3. A drawbridge.

SECTION IV.

1. In a musical-box, describe the mechanical contrivances (1) for making the barrel shift at the end of each tune, and (2) for controlling (1) so as to make it repeat the same tune.
2. Describe hinges that make a door self-closing, and explain carefully their action.
3. Describe a letter-weighing machine that shall always point exactly to the stamp to be used.

Section V.

Describe and explain the action of one of the following machines:

1. A sewing machine.
2. A weaver's loom.
3. A saw-mill.

Section VI.

1. Describe the process of manufacturing bar-iron.
2. Describe the construction of a Bramah's lock.
3. The gates in a lock are to be opened and closed by hydraulic machinery; describe what is required.

Section VII.

Describe and explain the action of one of the following machines:

1. A jack for roasting meat.
2. A windmill for grinding corn.
3. The steam plough.

Examination of Science Schools and Classes,
2nd May, 1862.

THEORETICAL MECHANICS.

General Instructions.

Three hours are allowed for this paper.

You are only permitted to attempt twelve questions.

You may select your questions from Series I., or from Series II., or from both.

The value attached to the correct answer of each question is marked against it.

N.B.—A full and correct construction will in all cases gain more marks than an inexact or incomplete one; though in the former case the question may be the more easy of the two and have less value attached to it.

Series I.

1. How do we measure "force" in Mechanics? What is a "lb. weight?" (10.)
2. A mass to be weighed when put into one scale of an untrue balance appears to weigh 12 lbs.; when put into the other scale it appears to be 14 lbs.; what is its true weight? (10.)
3. Find the centre of gravity of a solid formed of two unequal spheres touching each other. The radius of one is 4 inches, weight 10 lbs., the other, whose radius is 10 inches, weighs 20 lbs. (10.)
4. What would be the number expressing the force

of gravity, if one mile is the unit of length, and one minute the unit of time? (10.)

5. Write down the three laws of motion, and define *moving force*. (10.)
6. In a fluid at rest under the action of gravity, show that the pressure varies as the depth. (10.)
7. What will be the pressure on a horizontal square inch in a vessel of water, at a distance of 25 inches below the surface? (10.)
8. What must be the size of the surface pressed as in question 7, at a depth of 18 inches, when the pressure is exactly 1 lb.? (10.)
9. If a cylinder floats vertically in water, half immersed, what is its specific gravity? If now some fluid be mixed with the water so that the specific gravity of the mixture is 1·25, how much of the cylinder will be immersed? (12.)
10. How is the pressure of a given quantity of air enclosed in a vessel affected by raising the temperature? What is the law connecting pressure, density, and temperature in elastic fluids? (10.)
11. What are the conditions under which a body will be supported when resting on a horizontal plane? (10.)
12. A cone, radius of base = 2 inches, height = 8 inches, is placed on an inclined plane: determine the greatest inclination the plane can have before the cone topples over, supposing it to be prevented from sliding. (12.)

SERIES II.

13. If three forces represented in magnitude and

direction by the three sides of a triangle taken in order, act upon a point, they will keep it at rest. Assuming the law of the parallelogram of forces, prove this. (12.)

14. Four forces represented by 1, 2, 3, 4 lbs. taken in order act on a point in a plane, in directions at right angles to each other. Find the magnitude and direction of their resultant. (12.)

15. Show that when a body moves from rest under the action of an accelerating force (f), the velocity acquired being v in a space (s). $v^2 = fs$. (12.)

16. A body weighing 6 lbs. moving with a velocity of 10 feet per second meets directly a body of 8 lbs. moving with a velocity of 2 feet per second; their common elasticity is $\frac{1}{3}$. Find the motion of the bodies after impact. (12.)

17. When a body falls freely down a smooth inclined plane under the action of gravity from rest, it acquires a velocity equal to that which it would have acquired if it had fallen freely down the same vertical space. Prove this. (12.)

18. A cylindrical vessel, diameter of base 8 inches, height 12 inches, is filled with water. Find the whole pressure on the internal surface. (12.)

19. What is the *centre of pressure?* In a lock gate where the water reaches to the top of the gate, is the centre of pressure above, below, or coincident with the centre of gravity of the gate? Give reasons for your answer. (12.)

20. Hiero gave a goldsmith a certain weight of gold to make into a crown. When the crown was brought back, it weighed exactly the same weight as the gold which had been given. But

it was suspected that part of the gold had been replaced by an inferior metal. How did Archimedes discover the exact amount of the base metal? (12.)

21. A weight of 10 lbs. drags another weight of 8 lbs., the weights being connected by a string which passes over a fixed pulley, and both weights hanging vertically. At what rate does the centre of gravity of the weights descend? (16.)
22. What is meant by *centre of percussion?* (12.)
23. When a hole is made in the side of a vessel containing fluid, how can you determine the velocity of the efflux practically, to show that it is really equal to the theoretical velocity of efflux? (12.)
24. An elastic ball is dropped from a height of 10 feet on a horizontal plane. Its elasticity being $\frac{1}{5}$, find the whole space described before the motion ceases. (16.)

Examination of Science Schools and Classes,
3rd May, 1862.

APPLIED MECHANICS.

General Instructions.

Three hours are allowed for this paper.

You are only permitted to attempt ten questions.

You may select your questions from Series I., or from Series II., or from both.

The value attached to the correct answer of each question is marked against it.

N.B.—A full and exact answer will in all cases gain more marks than an inexact or incomplete one; though in the former case the question may be the more easy of the two and have less value attached to it.

Series I.

1. In the fastening of a sash-window, explain the use of the spring, the extent of its action, and the reason of the shape of each part of the contrivance. (16.)
2. Explain the construction of a good balance. (16.)
3. In using a pair of scissors, explain all the forces which are brought into action, showing by a diagram their directions. (16.)
4. A draw which has two handles has been pulled violently by *one* handle, and sticks fast. A chisel is given you to ease it; how will you use it? Give a diagram. (16.)
5. Describe a register, or tell-tale, by which toll-

takers at a bridge, or public exhibition, can be checked. (16.)

6. Explain the action of the fire-engine. (16.)
7. Describe the construction of the siphon used by distillers' workmen to draw the spirit from the cask on the dray without removing it, and explain its action. (16.)
8. What is the peculiar construction in the Bramah lock? Give a sketch of the works of a good lock for a cash-box. (16.)

SERIES II.

9. What are the different forms of common saws? Give reasons for the difference in construction. The shape of the teeth, and their *set* to be explained on mechanical principles. (16.)
10. Explain the action of the spring in a common pocket-knife. (16.)
11. How is a boat moved forward by means of a single paddle-oar, used at the stern? (16.)
12. What is the method of Sir W. Armstrong for making guns of forged iron? (16.)
13. Describe a screw-press. (16.)
14. If the action of an endless screw is reciprocal, *i. e.*, if it will act whether the wheel or the worm is driver, what limits must be assigned to the pitch of the screw? (16.)
15. Explain the construction of a dry gas-meter. Compare the relative advantages of dry and wet meters. (16.)
16. What is the construction of a common jack for roasting meat? (16.)

NOTE.—Good diagrams carefully sketched in plan, elevation, and section, will in all cases receive additional marks.

MECHANICAL PHYSICS.

PAPERS *given to Candidates in the Examination for Science Certificates, held at South Kensington, November*, 1862.

THEORETICAL MECHANICS.—1ST PAPER.

SECTION I.

1. How can a line represent a pressure? Under what condition will three pressures acting on a body keep it at rest?
2. Find the resultant of two pressures acting in parallel directions on a body, and define a statical couple.
3. Two small unequal spherical balls are put into a large hemispherical basin; when they are at rest draw all the pressures and indicate their directions. (No calculation required.)

SECTION II.

1. A workman sometimes uses his pickaxe as a lever. Explain the pressures called into action in such a case.
2 In using a pair of nutcrackers, what is the nature of the reaction at the hinge?
3. Why is it easier to carry two pails with a hoop keeping them asunder than it is to carry them alone in the same relative position? Explain the nature of the strain on the hoop.

SECTION III.

1. Define centre of gravity. Find that of a triangle.

2. A quadrilateral being traced upon paper, find its centre of gravity without a scale.
3. Find the centre of gravity of a solid formed by uniting a cylinder 4 inches long, diameter 2 inches; and a cone whose altitude is 4 inches, and diameter of base 2 inches; (1) when the base of the cone is applied to the base of the cylinder; (2) when the axes are in the same straight line and the vertex of the cone touches the centre of the base of the cylinder.

SECTION IV.

1. Explain the expressions "resistance of a surface," and "limiting angle of resistance."
2. Show that when a body rests on a horizontal plane, the smallest pressure that will bring it into a state bordering on motion will act in a direction inclined to the horizon at an angle equal to the limiting angle of resistance.
3. (P) hanging at A, balances (W) on F G, which is suspended by strings from d D. Find the relation of P : W, and show that if B d : D E :: B C : C E, it does not matter where W rests on the rod F G.

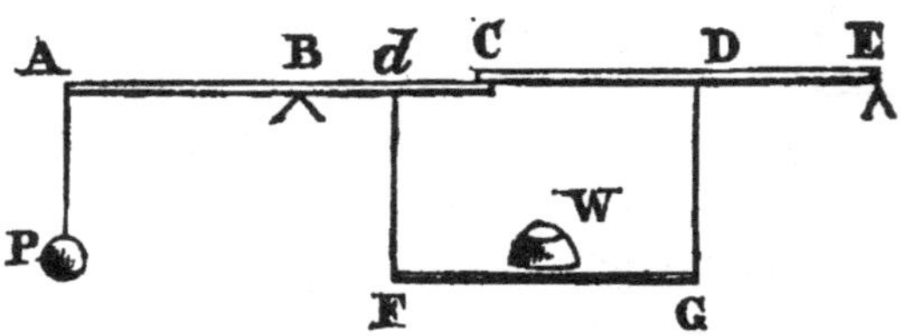

SECTION V.

1. Define *accelerating force, velocity, moving force.* State the second law of motion; how would you attempt to make it evident?

2. Through how many miles would a body falling freely from rest pass in the first minute?
3. A body is dropped from a height of 800 feet; at the same moment another is projected vertically upwards with a velocity of 150 feet per second where and when will they meet?

SECTION VI.

1. Show that the curve described by a projectile in a vacuum would be a parabola, whose axis is vertical.
2. A weight P is hanging over the edge of a table by a string, which is fastened to another weight W resting on the table. Find an expression for the accelerating force (1) when the table is smooth, (2) when it is rough. (The weight of the string to be neglected.)
3. Explain the principle of virtual velocities, and verify it in the case of two pressures in equilibrium on a straight bar capable of moving round a fixed point.

SECTION VII.

1. What is the nature of centrifugal force, and how is it measured?
2. What is meant by "work accumulated in a moving body?" Find an expression for it when a body is moving round a fixed axis.
3. Define "moment of inertia," "radius of gyration." If a heavy beam is revolving about an axis perpendicular to itself through one end, what is its radius of gyration?

SECTION VIII.

1. If a second's pendulum be carried one mile below

the surface of the earth, how many vibrations will it make in a day? (Take the earth's radius as 4000 miles, and consider it to be a sphere.)

2. What mechanical considerations show that the earth must be a figure different from a sphere?

3. A ball is suspended by an elastic string; suppose it suddenly pulled down through a small space, determine the time of vibration, and all the circumstances of the motion.

THEORETICAL MECHANICS.—2ND PAPER.

SECTION I.

1. How is mechanical "work" increased by the rigidity of ropes? Take the simple case of a single fixed pulley as an illustration.
2. What property of the cycloid renders it interesting in mechanics? How can a pendulum be made to vibrate in a cycloid?
3. What was the method adopted by Bessel to calculate the numerical value of the accelerating force of gravity?

SECTION II.

1. How would you show that pressure is transmitted by fluids in all directions without becoming diminished?
2. When two fluids that do not mix are placed in a bent tube whose parallel legs are vertical, show that the altitudes of the surfaces above the common surface of the fluids are inversely as the specific gravities of the fluids.
3. The pressure of a fluid on a surface wholly immersed in it is equal to the weight of a column of fluid whose base is the surface pressed, and altitude the depth of the centre of gravity of the surface. Prove this.

SECTION III.

1. A spherical ball, radius 2 inches, is wholly immersed in a fluid of specific gravity 1·47. Its centre is 5 inches below the surface. Find the whole pressure upon the sphere in ounces.

2. How is the "centre of pressure" defined, and how is it to be found in the case of a plane surface immersed in a fluid? (Indicate the method, without calculation.)
3. Prove that the depth of the centre of pressure of a rectangle one side of which is in the surface of a fluid is to the depth of the centre of gravity as 4 : 3.

SECTION IV.

1. When a body floats in a fluid, what are the laws of equilibrium? Prove them to be true.
2. What is the "metacentre" of a floating body? Why is a ship in ballast more stable than one with an empty hold? (Give a clear explanation without algebraic calculations.)
3. A small cylindrical cup (exterior dimensions, radius of base 2 inches, height 6 inches) whose weight is 2 ounces, floats in water. The thickness of the material is $\frac{1}{10}$ of an inch. How much mercury can be poured into it without causing it to sink? (Sp. gr. of mercury = 13·598.)

SECTION V.

1. What is an undulation? Explain "interference of waves."
2. How would you prove that "air has weight?"
3. What is a barometer? How is it constructed, and what are its chief uses? When the upper surface of the mercury sinks half an inch, is that the exact variation in the weight of the atmosphere?

SECTION VI.

1. Describe experiments which show the elastic force of air.
2. How can it be shown that the pressure of a gas is inversely proportional to the space it occupies?
3. Is the pressure of the atmosphere affected by the quantity of vapour it contains? How is that quantity ascertained?

SECTION VII.

1. When water issues from an orifice in the side of a vessel containing it, what is the form of the jet? By what means can the efflux be increased?
2. How can it be shown that air is necessary to the propagation of sound from one body to another? (No solid or liquid connecting them.)
3. What is the cause of the *Echo?* Illustrate your answer by a diagram.

SECTION VIII.

1. How would you show that friction takes place between solids and liquids, and between the particles of fluids themselves?
2. If a vessel containing fluid were made suddenly to rotate about a vertical axis, what form would the surface of the fluid assume? Give reasons for your answer.
3. Steam of pressure P lbs. to the square inch, is admitted into a cylinder of given dimensions, and drives the piston before it through one-third of the stroke; it is then cut off and left to work expansively. How is the work done to be calculated?

Subject II.—Applied Mechanics.

APPLIED MECHANICS.—1st Paper.

Section I.

1. What is the meaning of "modulus of elasticity?" The modulus of elasticity of copper wire being 17,000,000, determine the elongation of a wire 12 feet long, whose section is the $\frac{1}{100}$ part of a square inch, under a pressure of 100 lbs.
2. If 12 iron wires each $\frac{1}{10}$ of an inch in diameter just sustain a weight of 3 tons, what is the *tenacity* of iron wire?
3. What is the "modulus" of a machine? The diameter of the piston of an engine is 80 inches, the mean pressure of the steam 12 lbs. per square inch, the length of the stroke 10 feet, the number of strokes per minute is 10. It raises 50 cubic feet of water per minute from a depth of 250 fathoms. What is its modulus?

Section II.

1. How is the stability of a wall, subjected to given pressures, to be estimated? Give some simple illustration.
2. How is the pressure of earth against a revetment wall to be estimated? Give a diagram.
3. A wall of brickwork is to be built round a reservoir 20 feet deep, its slope is inward, it is 1 foot thick at the top and 10·74 feet thick at the bottom; when the reservoir is full the line of *resistance* will cut the base 6 inches within the

extrados. Show how the calculations are to be made.

SECTION III.

1. What is the "*Hunting Cog*" in toothed wheels? What is the object of introducing it?
2. What is the property of epicycloidal curves which makes them useful in drawing teeth of wheels? Define the curve, and prove the property in question.
3. A rack has to drive a pinion which carries pins; what is the proper form for the teeth of the rack? Give any other convenient form where the rack is the driver and the pinion the follower.

SECTION IV.

1. By what mechanical contrivance is the advance of the piece of timber in sawing machinery secured at the end of each stroke? Sketch it, and show the action.
2. Describe the "*Recoil*" escapement.
3. When motion round an axis is communicated to another axis at right angles to it, by bevil wheels, draw and describe a simple reversing motion. (The driving shaft is to turn constantly in the same direction, the other shaft to admit of instantaneous reversed motion.)

SECTION V.

1. Explain the construction of the *Fusee* in a watch.
2. Show a mechanical contrivance by which a shaft revolving uniformly may communicate a *variable* angular velocity to another shaft (admitting, in this case, of reversion).

3. Explain the combination called the *toggle joint.* Show how it is applied in the power-loom.

Section VI.

1. Explain the construction of the tubular girder.
2. What should be the shape of a beam of uniform strength throughout, when resting on two points of its extremities, it carries a given weight at a given point of it.
3. Where is the tendency to break greatest in a circular arch (1) loaded on the top; (2) when loaded at a given point?

Section VII.

1. What is the line of pressure in an arch of stone voussoirs? What two conditions must be fulfilled at the points where the line of pressure meets each joint in order to ensure equilibrium?
2. What is the form of a chain hung between two points? Give the chief properties of the curve.
3. In the preceding case, what is the tension at any point? Show that if a uniform chain hang freely over any two points, the extremities of the chain will lie in the same horizontal line, when the chain is in equilibrium.

APPLIED MECHANICS.—2ND PAPER.

SECTION I.

1. Give a simple account of the action of a common pump.
2. Explain the construction of the fire-engine.
3. Describe the construction and mode of action of a good air-pump, and calculate the density of the air left in the receiver after a given number of strokes.

SECTION II.

1. Explain the terms *overshot*, *undershot*, and *breast* wheel. Show how each one of them acts.
2. In an overshot wheel prove by calculation that a regular or uniform angular velocity is attained.
3. Describe the construction and action of *Barker's Mill*, or the *Turbine*.

SECTION III.

1. Explain the action of the siphon. When the surface of the water has sunk to the level of the extremity of the shorter leg, what becomes of the water in the siphon?
2. Describe the action of the *Spiral Pump*, or *Zurich Machine*.
3. Explain the action of the hydraulic ram, and show how the same principle acts in the suction ram.

SECTION IV.

1. Explain the construction of Nicholson's hydrometer. Show how it must be used to compare the specific gravity of a liquid and of a solid.

2. Explain the construction and action of the *Stereometer* for measuring the volumes of small solids which cannot be immersed in water.
3. Describe and draw the marine screw propeller, and explain its action.

SECTION V.

Describe and draw one of the following machines:
1. A steam hammer.
2. A jib crane.
3. A common clock.

SECTION VI.

Describe and draw one of the following machines:
1. A foot-lathe.
2. A punching machine.
3. A marine steam engine.

SECTION VII.

1. Describe a self-registering barometer.
2. What are the chief results of experiments to ascertain the amount of resistance offered by water to moving bodies?
3. Explain the difference between the phenomena of tides in rivers and in the open seas. What is the "*Establishment of a Port?*" In some places there are *four* tides in twenty-four hours: how can this be explained?

Examination of Science Schools and Classes, 4th May, 1863.

THEORETICAL MECHANICS.

General Instructions.

Three hours are allowed for this paper.

You are only permitted to attempt twelve questions.

You may select your questions from Series I., or from Series II., or from both.

The value attached to the correct answer of each question is marked against it.

N.B.—A full and correct answer will in all cases gain more marks than an inexact or incomplete one; though in the former case the question may be the more easy of the two and have less value attached to it.

Series I.

1. When two weights placed on a straight lever are inversely as their distances from the fulcrum, show that they will balance. (10.)
2. Weights of 15 lbs. and 8 lbs. are connected by a uniform rod which weighs 1 lb. and is 12 inches long. Find the point in the rod where it must be suspended, that the weights may balance each other. (10.)
3. An equilateral triangle is divided into two parts by a line parallel to one side through the centre of gravity of the triangle: find the centre of gravity of the quadrilateral portion of it. (10.)
4. A mass of 4 tons moving with a velocity of 7 yards per second, meets directly a mass of 6

tons moving with a velocity of 4 feet per second. Supposing the bodies inelastic, how much velocity is lost by the first mass? (10.)

5. A body is thrown vertically downwards with a velocity of 10 feet per second; it reaches the ground in 12 seconds. What space has it described? (10.)

6. A vessel is full of water, a piece of wood weighing 3 lbs. is placed in it and floats: how many cubic inches of water will run over? (10.)

7. A cubical box whose side is 10 inches floats in water, its weight is 10 ounces; neglecting the thickness of the material, how much mercury (specific gravity 13·6) can be poured in, before the water overflows the edges of the box? (10.)

8. Explain clearly the conditions of *weight* and *position* when a body floats in a fluid. (10.)

9. A cylindrical jar, 6 inches in height, full of air, is forced with its mouth downwards in water till the mouth is at a depth of 8 feet: how high will the water rise in the jar? (10.)

10. Describe some simple experiments to show that the pressure of air is increased by heat. (10.)

11. What is a *horse power?* How many horse powers will it take to raise 4 cwt. per minute from a pit whose depth is 80 fathoms? (10.)

12. Describe a simple experiment (without an air-pump) to show that all bodies would fall to the ground in the same time through the same height, if it were not for the resistance of the air. (10.)

SERIES II.

1. When two forces act in any direction on the arms

of a bent lever, and keep it at rest, find by a geometrical construction the magnitude and direction of the pressure of the fulcrum. (20.)

2. In the preceding case, suppose the lever *straight*, and not attached to the fulcrum, what conditions are necessary to ensure equilibrium? (20.)

3. A circular table resting on three legs under its edge, and equally distant from each other, weighs 60 lbs., what is the least weight which, resting on the edge of the table, can overturn it? (20.)

4. When a billiard-ball moving with a given velocity in a given direction meets the cushion, show how, by geometrical construction, we can discover the direction and velocity of the ball after reflexion. (20.)

5. Explain the action of a pendulum, and show that the time of vibration is proportional to the square root of the length. (20.)

6. A cone of wood whose axis is 8 inches and radius of base 2 inches, floats in water with its axis vertical. If its specific gravity be ·8, how much of the axis is immersed? (20.)

7. A B C is a tube bent so that the legs are parallel; being held vertically upwards 8 cubic inches of mercury are poured into C, and 12 cubic inches of water into A (the section of the tube being 1 square inch). Find the distances between the upper surfaces of the water and mercury, and their common surface. The horizontal part is 2 inches long. (20.)

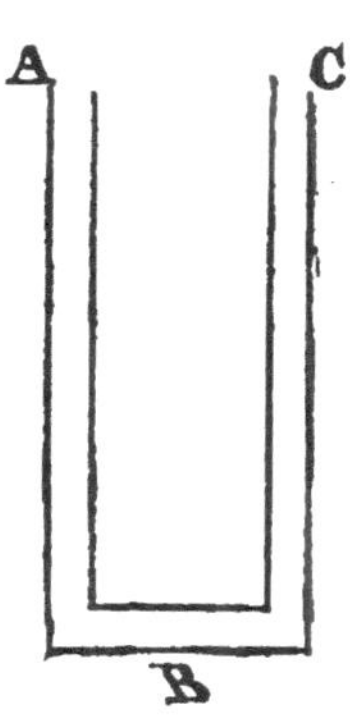

8. When a hollow sphere, radius 5 inches, is filled with water, what is the whole pressure on the internal surface? Compare this pressure with the weight of the water. (20.)

9. With what velocity must a heavy body be projected downwards that in 8" it may overtake another which was dropped 3" before it? (20.)

10. A pendulum which vibrates seconds at the earth's surface is taken down a mine which is one mile deep. Will it gain or lose, and how many seconds in a day? Take the earth's radius equal to 4000 miles. (20.)

11. Explain what is meant by *wave motion*. (20.)

12. What mechanical considerations determined the form to be given to the fusee of a watch? What is that form? What are the mechanical properties of the curve? (20.)

Examination of Science Schools and Classes,
5th May, 1863.

APPLIED MECHANICS.

General Instructions.

Three hours are allowed for this paper.

You are only permitted to attempt seven questions.

You may select your questions from Series I., or from Series II., or from both.

The value attached to the correct answer of each question is marked against it.

N.B.—A full and exact answer will in all cases gain more marks than an inexact or incomplete one; though in the former case the question may be the more easy of the two and have less value attached to it.

Series I.

1. How are railway tickets stamped with the date of their issue? Mention other instances where the same mechanical contrivance is used. (15.)
2. Describe the lock of a gun, and the uses of the several parts. (15.)
3. Describe the slide valve of a steam engine, and show how its motion is governed by the engine-shaft. (15.)
4. Explain all the mechanical contrivances between the handle at the street door and the clapper of a house bell. (15.)
5. Describe a spirit-level, and explain its principle. (15.)

6. How is the action of intermittent springs explained on hydrostatical principles? (15.)
7. How is the railway-whistle constructed? (15.)
8. What is the principle of the washing-machine, or the knife-cleaner? (15.)

Series II.

1. The bow and stern of a boat are attached by long ropes to a stake in the middle of a rapid stream. How can a man manage to pass from one side to the other by their means, without oar or paddle? (30.)

   Full explanation required.
2. How is the tendency of a locomotive to fly off when going round a curve, counteracted? (30.)

   Full explanation required, with calculation.
3. Explain the action of the capstan. (30.)
4. How is the speed of a steam engine made to regulate itself? Explain contrivances, with sketches. (30.)
5. Explain the construction of the hand mowing machine for lawns. (30.)
6. Explain the action of the marine screw propeller. (30.)
7. Show how an inkstand may be constructed so as to give a constant supply, and preserve the ink as much as possible from dust and evaporation. (30.)
8. Describe an instrument for comparing the specific gravity of fluids, or of a solid and a fluid, and illustrate its action by examples. (30.)

APPENDIX.

The following examples, chosen from the preceding examination papers, have been worked as specimens of the way in which the principle of mechanics are applied to the solution of problems.

May, 1861. *Series I.* 2.

Let A B represent the rod, and C its middle point
Let T = tension of the string at A
And T′ = " " " B

The weight of the rod, which is 2 lbs., may be supposed to be collected at its centre of gravity C.

Take the 10 lbs. as 2 feet 6 inches from A. Then taking A as a fulcrum, we have

$$T' \times AB = 2 \times AC + 10 \times 2\tfrac{1}{2}$$

$$12\,T' = 37$$

$$T' = \frac{37}{12} = 3\tfrac{1}{12} \text{ lbs.}$$

Similarly, by taking B as a fulcrum, T may be found.

Series II. 16.

The downward pressure of the 6 lbs. parallel to the plane is found from the following proportion :

$$\text{Height} : \text{length} :: P : W$$
$$= 1 : 3 :: P : 6$$
$$\therefore P = 2 \text{ lbs.} = \text{the portion of the}$$

6 lbs. which is dragged by the 4 lbs. weight.

Then we have

The moving force $= 4 - 2$

„ weight moved $= 4 + 6$

and since $W : P :: g : f$

$$f, \text{ or accelerating force} = \frac{4-2}{4+6} g = \tfrac{1}{5} \times \frac{322}{10}$$
$$= 6\tfrac{11}{25}$$

To determine T, or the tension of the string:

The moving force on the 6 lbs. will be $T - 2$

and the accelerating force $\dfrac{T-2}{6} g$

Similarly accelerating force downwards on the 4 lbs.

$$= \frac{4-T}{4} g$$

The string being considered inextensible, these quantities must be equal:

$$\therefore \frac{T-2}{6} g = \frac{4-T}{4} g$$
$$\therefore 4T - 8 = 24 - 6T$$
$$T = 3\tfrac{1}{5}$$

Section III. 1. (*2nd Paper.*)

Let x and y = sp. gravities of fresh and salt water respectively

and V = volume of salt water displaced

then $V + An =$ „ fresh „ „

$\therefore Vy$ = weight of salt water displaced

and $(V+A\,n)\,x =$ weight of fresh water displaced

$$\therefore V\,y = (V+A\,n)\,x$$

$$\therefore V\,(y - x) = A\,n\,x$$

$$\therefore V = \frac{A\,n\,x}{y-x}$$

$$\therefore \text{weight of salt water displaced} = \frac{A\,n\,x\,y}{y-x}$$

$$\therefore \text{weight of ship} = \frac{A\,n\,x\,y}{y-x}$$

Section V. 1.

Weight of metal in vacuo $= 3$ lbs.

" " water $= 2\frac{3}{4}$ lbs.

$\therefore$ " water displaced $= \frac{1}{4}$ lb.

$$\therefore \frac{\text{sp. gravity of metal}}{\text{sp. gravity of water}} = \frac{3}{\frac{1}{4}} = \frac{12}{1}$$

Weight of water displaced by compound $= 5 - 1\frac{1}{2} = 3\frac{1}{2}$

" " " metal $= 3 - 2\frac{3}{4} = \frac{1}{4}$

" " " wood $= 3\frac{1}{2} - \frac{1}{4} = 3\frac{1}{4}$

and weight of wood $= 2$ lbs. in vacuo

$$\therefore \frac{\text{sp. gravity of wood}}{\text{sp. gravity of water}} = \frac{2}{3\frac{1}{4}} = \frac{\cdot\dot{6}1538\dot{4}}{1}$$

Hence, taking sp. gravity of water as the standard, the sp. gravities of the wood and metal are $\cdot\dot{6}1538\dot{4}$ and 12.

May 2, 1862. *Series I.* 12.

Let A B C be the plane, A B being the length, D E F the cone, and G its centre of gravity. It will be on the point of toppling over when the vertical line G E from G, its centre of gravity, passes through E, which represents the circumference of the base.

Let H be the point where the line from the vertex, passing through G, meets the base. Then we have

$$EH = 2\text{ in.} = GH$$

and the angle at H is a right angle, and the angle HGE = the angle HEG

∴ each of them is half a right angle

Produce GE to meet the base of the plane in K.

Then the angle at K is a right angle

and the angle BEK is half a right angle

∴ the angle at B is half a right angle

which is the greatest inclination that can be given to the plane to prevent the cone from falling over.

Series II. 16.

Let M, M′ = masses of bodies respectively

V, V′ = velocities of bodies respectively before impact

v, v' = velocities after impact

R, R′ = forces of compression and restitution

$$\text{then } R' = \frac{R}{3}$$

$$v = V - \frac{4}{3} \cdot \frac{M'}{M+M'}(V+V') = 10 - \frac{4}{3} \times \frac{8}{14} \times \frac{12}{1} = \frac{6}{7}$$

$$v' = -V' + \frac{4}{3} \cdot \frac{M}{M+M'}(V+V') = -2 \times \frac{4}{3} \times \frac{6}{14} \times \frac{12}{1} = \frac{34}{7}$$

∴ the velocities after impact are in the direction of the first ball, and are respectively $\frac{6}{7}$ feet, $\frac{34}{7}$ feet, per second.

November, 1862. *Section III.* 3. (*1st Paper.*)

In the first case, the centre of gravity of the cone is 1 inch from the common base; the centre of gravity of the cylinder is 2 inches from the common base, and the line joining these is coincident with the axes of the cone and cylinder.

Let G be the centre of gravity required, and let g, g' be the centres of gravity of the cone and cylinder respectively.

Then, distance of G from g : distance of G from g' :: weight of cylinder : weight of cone :: 3 : 1.

$\therefore$ G is distant from g, $\frac{3}{4}$ of 3 in. $= 2\frac{1}{4}$ in.
and G is distant from g', $\frac{1}{4}$ of 3 in. $= \frac{3}{4}$ in.
or G is distant from the common base $1\frac{1}{4}$ in.

In the second case, the distance $g\,g' = 5$ in.
and G will be distant from g, $3\frac{3}{4}$ in.
or from the point of contact $\frac{3}{4}$ in.

Section IV. 3.

Let t, t' be the tensions of strings F d, G D
Let R be the mutual pressure at C
And k the position of W on F G

$$\text{Then, } P.\,AB = t.\,Bd + R.\,BC \quad \text{(i.)}$$
$$t'\,DE = R.\,CE \quad \text{(ii.)}$$
$$t'\,kG = t.\,Fk \quad \text{(iii.)}$$
$$W = t + t'. \quad \text{(iv.)}$$

From i. and ii. we get $P.\,AB = t.Bd + t'\frac{DE}{CE}\cdot BC$

substituting iii. we get $P.\,AB = t\left(Bd + \frac{Fk}{kG}\cdot\frac{DE}{CE}\cdot BC\right)$

by iii. and iv. $W = t\left(1 + \frac{Fk}{kG}\right)$

$$\therefore \frac{P}{W} = \frac{Bd.\,kG.\,CE + Fk.\,DE.\,BC}{AB\,(kG.\,CE + Fk.\,CE} \quad 5$$

If $Bd : DE :: BC : CE$, then $Bd.\,CE = DE.\,BC$, and 5 becomes

$$\frac{P}{W} = \frac{DE.\,BC}{FG.\,AB}, \text{ where } k \text{ vanishes.}$$

Section VIII. 1.

Let t, t' = times of vibration at the earth's surface and below it.

Let g, g' = force of gravity at the earth's surface and below it.

$$\text{Then } t : t' :: \pi\sqrt{\frac{l}{g}} : \pi\sqrt{\frac{l}{g'}}$$

$$:: \frac{1}{\sqrt{g}} : \frac{1}{\sqrt{g^1}}$$

$$:: \sqrt{g^1} : \sqrt{g}$$

$$\text{and } g : g^1 :: 4000 : 3999$$

$$\therefore t^2 : t'^2 :: 3999 : 4000$$

$$\therefore t'^2 = \frac{4000}{3999} = 1{\cdot}00025$$

$$t' = 1{\cdot}00012$$

$\therefore$ number of vibrations in 24 hours

$$= \frac{24 \times 60 \times 60}{1{\cdot}00012} = \frac{86400}{1{\cdot}00012} = 86389{\cdot}6$$

May 4, 1863. *Series II.* 7.

When the mercury has been poured in, it will stand at the same height—3 inches—in each limb.

When the water has been poured in, the weight of the mercury in the right limb must be equal to the weight of the mercury in the left + weight of water.

Let x = number of cubic in. of mercury in the right limb.

Then $8-(x+2)=6-x$ = number in the left

Taking the weight of water as unity, we have

$$13{\cdot}58\,x=12+13{\cdot}58\,(6-x)$$
$$27{\cdot}16\,x=93{\cdot}48$$
$$\therefore x=3\,\frac{300}{679}\text{ cubic in.}$$

And since the section of the tube is 1 square inch, this will be the height of the mercury in the right limb — also the height of that in the left limb $=2\,\frac{379}{679}$ in.

$\therefore$ height of the surface of the water is $14\,\frac{379}{679}$ in.

The distance between the upper surfaces is

$$14\,\frac{379}{679}-3\,\frac{300}{679}=11\,\frac{79}{679}\text{ in.}$$

And the common surface of the water and mercury is $2\,\frac{300}{679}$ inches from the bottom of the left tube.

Section V. 3.

Let t = number of seconds after projection before they meet.

In t seconds the first body descends $\frac{1}{2} g t^2$ feet, and the second ascends $(V t - \frac{1}{2} g t^2)$ feet. The sum of these is 800 feet; that is

$$\tfrac{1}{2} g t^2 + V t - \tfrac{1}{2} g t^2 = 800 \text{ ft.}$$

$$\therefore V t = 800 \text{ ft.}$$

$$t = \frac{800}{150} = 5\tfrac{1}{3} \text{ sec.}$$

ANSWERS TO EXAMPLES.

THE LEVER.

2. $9\frac{1}{5}$ in.
3. $36\frac{3}{17}$ lbs.
4. $3\frac{19}{56}$ in.
5. $288\frac{51}{56}$ in.
6. $3\frac{39}{56}$ in.
7. $15\frac{3}{7}$ lbs.
8. $166\frac{2}{3}$ oz.
9. 24 cwt.
10. Yes, if weight of board is less than his weight.
11. 720 lbs.
12. 4 lbs.
13. $2\frac{2}{3}$ lbs.
14. 36 lbs.
15. 10 in.
16. 3 lbs.
17. $18\frac{2}{7}$ inches from the smaller weight.
18. $18\frac{2}{3}$ inches from the smaller weight.
19. 22 lbs. and 14lbs.
20. 81. in.
21. No.
22. Yes.
23. $9\frac{1}{3}$.
24. 15 stone and 12 stone.
25. 5 feet from the man supporting 24 lbs.
26. 79 in.
27. $6\frac{6}{13}$ in.
28. 3 in.
29. 20 in.
30. $47\frac{1}{2}$ cwts.
31. 5 : 4.

31(*a*). 7 : 5.

32. 84 lbs.
33. $1\frac{5}{9}$ tons.
34. 36 cwts.
35. 90 in.
36. 1 ft. 9 inches.

36 (*a*). 1 yd. 2 ft. $8\frac{2}{5}$ in.

37. 1 ft. 4 in.
38. $4\frac{2}{7}$ lbs.
39. 6 lbs.
40. 64 lbs. and 48 lbs.

40 (*a*). $22\frac{2}{33}$ lbs. and $33\frac{31}{33}$ lbs.

41. $4\frac{1}{2}$ ft from one end.

41 (*a*). $2\frac{2}{11}$ ft. from end with less pressure.

42. 3 ft. 1 in.

43. $85\frac{1}{3}$ lbs. and $77\frac{1}{3}$ in.
43 (*a*). 1 lb. $6\frac{2}{13}$ oz. : $6\frac{2}{13}$ oz.
44. The former.
44 (*a*). The former.
45. $4\frac{114}{179}$ ft. and $5\frac{65}{179}$ ft.
45 (*a*). $6\frac{69}{101}$ ft. from heavier boy.
46. 2nd, 1st, 2nd, 1st.
47. 56 ft.
48. 6 cwts.
49. 5 lbs.
50. 3 qrs.
51. 6 and 10.
52. 20 in.
53. 320 lbs. and 128 lbs.
53 (*a*). 1 cwt. 3 qrs. $5\frac{3}{5}$ lbs. and 1 cwt. 0 qrs. $22\frac{2}{5}$ lbs.
54. $\frac{1}{4}$ length of lever.
55. 10, 39, &c. oz.
55 (*a*). 8·04674 oz.
56. $14\frac{2}{5}$ in. and $21\frac{3}{5}$ in.
56 (*a*). $4\frac{8}{13}$ in. from greater weight.
57. $19\frac{1}{2}$ in.
58. 2 in. from the middle on the 7 lbs. side.
58 (*a*). $5\frac{1}{3}$ in. from 7 lbs. weight.
58 (*b*). $5\frac{1}{3}$ in. from 7 lbs. weight.
58 (*c*). $20\frac{5}{11}$ in. from 9 lbs. weight.
59. 3 : 2.

Wheel and Axle.

2. 6 in.
3. 40 lbs.
4. $2\frac{1}{3}$ cwt.
5. 2 qrs. $25\frac{5}{18}$ lbs.
6. $222\frac{43}{69}$ lbs.
7. 3 in.
8. 28 lbs.
9. $P = 3\frac{3}{4}$ lbs.; $W = 6\frac{1}{4}$ lbs.
10. $P - 432$ lbs., therefore 4 men must be employed.
11. 8 lbs.
12. $1\frac{7}{8}$ lbs.
13. 6 ft. 2 in.
14. 2 in.
15. 30 cwt. 24 lbs.
16. 10 : 11.
17. 1 cwt. 1 qr. 20 lbs.
18. 30 lbs.
19. 5 cwt.
20. $61\frac{1}{11}$ lbs.
21. 7 cwt. 2 qrs. 10 lbs.
22. $35\frac{5}{7}$ lbs.
23. 72 lbs.
24. $9\frac{1}{3}$ lbs.

25. 1 ft. 2 in.
26. 1 : 10.
27. 29 cwt. 1 qr. $7\frac{1}{5}$ lbs.
28. $283\frac{1}{2}$.
29. $24\frac{1}{2}$ in.

Pulleys.

2 (*a*). 36 lbs.
3. 35.3 lbs.
4. 72 cwt.
5. 450 lbs.
6. 50.
7. 314 lbs.
8. 6.
9. 48 lbs.
10. 10 ft.
11. 15 men.
12. $2\frac{1}{4}$ ft.
13. 18 feet.
14. 7 lbs.
15. $\frac{7x}{8}$ lbs.
16. A power of 2.
17. 140 lbs.
18. 272 lbs.
19. 157·5 lbs.
20. 20 lbs.
21. 14 oz.
22. 72 times the space of W.
23. 36 lbs.
24. 56 lbs.
25. 3 lbs.
26. 18 lbs.
27. 34 lbs.
28. 5.
29. Motion will take place in the direction of the power.
30. 105 lbs.
31. 320 lbs.

Wheels and Pinions.

2. $1\frac{1}{2}$ in.
3. $8\frac{16}{23}$ lbs.
4. 35351 : 182
5. 36 lbs.
6. $6273\frac{17}{23}$ lbs.

Inclined Plane.

3. 3 lbs.
4. $214\frac{2}{9}$ lbs.
5. $10\frac{1}{2}$ ft.
6. $6\frac{1}{4}$ in.
7. $12\frac{1}{2}$ lbs.
8. 108 lbs.

9. 3 qrs. 14 lbs.
10. $2\frac{3}{4}$ ft.
11. $2\frac{1}{4}$ lbs.
12. 21 lbs.
13. 6 lbs.
14. 56 lbs.
15. 15 lbs.
16. $385\frac{5}{6}$ lbs.
17. 6 ft. $7\frac{57}{173}$ in.
18. $\frac{1}{2}$ cwt.
19. 1 : 6.
20. 7 cwt.
21. 28 lbs.
22. $146\frac{1}{2}$ lbs.
23. $\frac{27}{28}$ in.
24. 80 ft.
25. $15\frac{1}{3}$ cwt.
26. $67\frac{1}{2}$ lbs.
27. $1\frac{1}{2}$ tons.
28. 1 ton 19 cwt. 3 qrs.
22.3958 lbs.
30. 51.423008 lbs.
31. 7.4162 oz.
32. 4 lbs.
33. 1 : 3.

Screw.

1. 1716 lbs.
2. 85·6 lbs.
3. 120 lbs.
4. 9·9 lbs.
5. 1·3793 cwts.
6. 285·1.
7. 4·45 lbs.
8. 6·6 lbs.
9. 1·8 lbs.
10. 18095·6 lbs.
11. 11·88 lbs.
12. 18849·6 lbs.
13. 4523·904 lbs.
14. 143257 lbs.
15. 119 :: 38 :: 1.
16. 603·18.
17. 4825·49 lbs.
18. 11·8 lbs.
19. 16964·64 lbs.
20. ·439824 in.
21. 224 lbs.
22. 1 : 240.
23. 2000 lbs.

Composition and Resolution of Forces.

2. 16.
3. 34.
4. 28.
5. 65·9.
6. 57·5.
7. $6\sqrt{5}$; $12\sqrt{5}$.
8. 35·44.
9. 43·4.

Falling Bodies.

1. 400 ft.
2. 13456 ft.
3. 784 ft.
4. 96 ft.
5. 176 ft.
6. 256 ft.
7. 208 ft.
8. 144 ft.
9. 144 ft.
10. 400 ft.
11. 256 ft.
12. 144 ft.
13. 64 ft.
14. 576 ft.
15. 18 ft.
16. 4.4 secs.
17. 9·0625 secs.
18. 224 ft.
19. 3·74 secs.
20. 1024 ft.
21. 288 ft.
22. 324 ft.
23. 6·25 secs.
24. 23963·04 ft.
25. 9·08 secs. 290·56 ft.
26. 100 ft.
27. (1.) 243.36 ft.
    (2.) 186 ft.
28. 196 ft.
30. 1024 ft.
31. 36 ft.
32. 484 feet ; 11 secs.

Momentum.

(Unit of weight, 1 lb. ; of space, 1 foot ; of time, 1 sec.)

1. 30.
2. 394240.
3. 4200.
4. 180.
5. $\frac{5}{2}$ lbs.
6. 900.
7. 788480.
8. 1140.
9. 1140.
10. 36 lbs.
13. $38\frac{2}{5}$ lbs.
14. $21\frac{2}{3}$ lbs.
15. $2\frac{3}{4}$ lbs.
16. 30 ft.
17. $239\frac{1}{5}$ feet resulting velocity.
18. $2779\frac{7}{17}$ ft.
19. $11\frac{71}{121}$ feet velocity ; earth's M^m 1440 ; comet's $M^m = 38$.
20. $\frac{8}{31}$ v. in direction of A.
21. Comet's velocity $2\frac{4}{7}$.
22. 200 lbs.
23. $3\frac{5}{13}$ feet velocity in direction of A.
24. $25\frac{201}{1529}$ ft.
25. 35 and 1500.
26. $21\frac{7}{13}$.

Sound.

1. 5600 ft.
2. 3360 ft.
3. 3360 ft.
4. 1680 ft.

Specific Gravity.

1. 1·528.
2. 4.
3. $4225\frac{1}{2}$ oz.
4. 7986 oz.
5. ·8235.
6. 4228 oz.
7. 40500.
8. ·8363.
9. ·8802.
10. 8·174.
11. 8·225.
12. 15529·7 oz.
13. ·2903.
14. 1·593.
15. 8·842.
16. $480\frac{19}{32}$ oz.

THE END.

CPSIA information can be obtained
at www.ICGtesting.com
Printed in the USA
LVHW091514230322
714114LV00005B/196

9 783752 585285